SEEKING SHELTER

To my friend Deb,
Enjoy reading!
Cathey

Seeking SHELTER

Catherine Goodwin

RONSDALE PRESS

RONSDALE PRESS
3350 West 21st Avenue
Vancouver, B.C., Canada V6S 1G7
www.ronsdalepress.com

Typesetting: Julie Cochrane, in Minion 12 pt on 16
Cover Art: James Bentley
Cover Design: Julie Cochrane
Paper: Ancient Forest Friendly Rolland "Enviro" — 100% post-consumer
    waste, totally chlorine-free and acid-free

Ronsdale Press wishes to thank the Canada Council for the Arts, the Government of Canada through the Book Publishing Industry Development Program (BPIDP), and the Province of British Columbia through the British Columbia Arts Council for their support of its publishing program.

Library and Archives Canada Cataloguing in Publication

Goodwin, Catherine
    Seeking shelter / Catherine Goodwin.

    ISBN-10: 1-55380-033-8
    ISBN-13: 978-1-55380-033-0

    1. Homeless women — Québec (Province) — Montréal — Juvenile fiction.
I. Title.

PS8613.O6483S43 2006   jC813'.6   C2005-907739-5

At Ronsdale Press we are committed to protecting the environment. To this end we are working with Markets Initiative (www.oldgrowthfree.com) and printers to phase out our use of paper produced from ancient forests. This book is one step towards that goal.

Printed in Canada by AGMV Marquis

To Janet and Carole
in memory of our mother,
Robina Campbell

Chapter one

"**I** can't, Dad. I can't go alone. Not back there!"

I tried to explain about the memories, about Mom, about Daniella.

"I don't want to go," I pleaded, but Dad just didn't get it. How had he put it?

"Chance to sort things out, Marcie," he'd said as though we were talking about the week's wash instead of my whole summer. That's Dad for you, missing the whole point and never listening to anyone else.

Mom wasn't like that.

I can't . . . can't go . . . go back.

The conversation stuck in my brain, joined now by the clacking of train wheels as they counted down the distance into the city. I sat ramrod straight, folding and unfolding my hands. Dad had won, but then he usually did. That's his way.

I heard the low bawl of the train whistle announce our approach.

"MONTREAL!"

The word squeezed through an intercom on the ceiling and rattled around our train car. If anyone had told me how hard this would be, I'd never have believed it.

Dad writes for a magazine in Toronto. Every couple of months he's sent on some hotshot assignment and when it comes to a story — he goes. Most of the kids I know in Toronto are away, so Dad is sending me to the Crieffs' house for the summer. Daniella Crieff was a neighbour and my best friend once, but that was long ago.

I sprung up, swaying with the motion of the train and dragged my knapsack and violin from the overhead rack. The passenger beside me glanced at his watch.

"There's no rush," he said. "We still have a few minutes."

"I know," I mumbled, sinking into the seat and tucking my bags close to my legs. It was getting dark and I could barely see the two-storey homes flashing by beside the track. My own image appeared in the glass. I glanced from the mass of dark curls in the window to the baggy knees of my jeans. What would Daniella look like now?

As the train rumbled through communities outside Montreal, I forced myself to focus on the lights. I'd discovered awhile ago, passing the brick buildings of John Abbott College, that staring at something in the distance held back the tears.

John Abbott was where Mom and I used to have picnics. We would drive out to Ste-Anne-de-Bellevue, then walk along Lakeshore Drive and end up at the College for lunch.

Flattening myself against the rough fabric of the seat, I slumped down until only my head showed in the glass. It was hard to go back.

A woman across the aisle opened her eyes and smiled. She'd slept since Toronto, but as we crept into the city she sat up and applied a thick layer of red to her mouth. Sucking inward, she slid her lips back and forth a few times then plunked the lipstick into her bag.

"Are you from Montreal?"

"No," I lied and looked out the window, hoping she'd stop talking to me.

It worked.

As the train inched forward, I heard only my heart in my ears. We were a few minutes from Central Station and a few minutes from Daniella, my former best friend.

It was now almost four years since we moved out of Montreal.

Nearly four years since Dad sold our home and we left for Toronto.

It's been exactly four years since Mom died.

And this is my first trip back.

I thought I'd see the Crieffs at the people-rush-to-meet-you level, but I didn't. My eyes darted around the station. Not one person rushed toward me. I kept expecting Daniella to call out my name, but no one did.

"... *Oui, vas-y* ... *non* ... *pas ici* ..."

Omigosh! No one spoke English. That had never bothered me before. Now I clutched onto the few words I understood, repeating and translating in my head. French inside my classroom seemed slower, easier to understand than the words out here, galloping around the station. What the heck was Dad thinking sending me here?

"Search for your strength," he had said when I'd boarded the train over four hours ago. Dad loves words.

I stood on my tiptoes straining to see. The few travellers I recognized from my train were leaving. Everyone hugged someone or hurried out of the station, knowing exactly which direction to take.

"Excuse me, *excuse,* do you know where a phone is?" I asked a custodian mopping the floor.

"Eh?"

"Phones? Do you know where the public phones are?"

The man looked around. He tried to answer my question, repeating something, pointing toward wickets before going back to work. The ammonia-scented cleanser he used stung my nose and my eyes.

"Now, they'll think I'm crying," I said aloud, but I don't think anyone heard me or cared.

Wiping my eyes with the sleeve of my shirt, I searched for the phones myself and spotted a few near a small bakery counter. I wriggled out of my backpack and put down my violin. Why had I dragged that thing along? It was small for me now, but Dad had insisted. Eight weeks, he said, was too long without practice.

"Marcie?"

I recognized Mrs. Crieff's voice before I saw her hurrying toward me. Daniella was behind, hanging back a little. She wore black shorts and a t-shirt.

"Good to see you, Marcie," Mrs. Crieff said, putting a soft, cool cheek on mine. I heard her kiss rather than felt it. She smelled good. Like vanilla. Mrs. Crieff gently nudged Daniella forward with the palm of her hand. "You remember Marcie, don't you?" she prompted. "Your little friend across the street."

"Um-hmm," Daniella mumbled. She raised a shoulder, flicking away her mother's hand. Poor Daniella. That's the sort of thing Dad would do.

"Hi," I said, glancing at my former friend then quickly down at my shoes. Daniella looked tall and so thin. Her hair, cropped like a boy's, had long straight bangs blonder than the rest. She wore gold stud earrings and had a small hoop pierced high on one ear.

"The car's out this way," Mrs. Crieff said, nodding toward an exit.

"Okay," I answered, trying to smile. My top lip caught

onto my braces and stuck there. Daniella stared. I thought I might've seen a slight curve at the corner of her mouth, but maybe not. As I picked up my bags, she flipped back her bangs, then dragged along quite a bit behind us.

All the way to the Crieffs' house, blue, violet and gold neon signs flickered outside our car. The city seemed to be running along beside us, poking its huge head into the window and humming something into my ears.

"How was your trip down, Marcie?" Mrs. Crieff asked. She didn't turn her head, but I saw her eyes framed in the rearview mirror, searching my face.

"All right," I answered. "It was a bit long."

The car slowed on an incline and I glanced outside. We'd started toward Mount Royal. There, bleached in city lights, was the hospital. A massive brick building that had gobbled up nearly a block since the last time I'd been there. The night that my mother had died.

I sank my teeth into my bottom lip and stared at the back of Daniella's seat.

"Were you waiting long, Marcie?" Mrs. Crieff interrupted my thoughts.

"No, not long."

"We were afraid you'd think we weren't coming."

"We were?" Daniella mumbled through a hand covering part of her mouth and most of her cheek. It was the first thing she had said since we drove out of the parking lot. She laughed then and added, "Just kidding."

What had I liked about her? I tried to remember, but couldn't.

We drove in silence for awhile. It was such a creepy feeling being back. As we passed my old school, I noticed a new chain-linked fence surrounding the yard. That's where I'd first met Daniella. She was a grade ahead of me and never spoke when her school friends were around. Sometimes she shot baskets with me though, and we always walked home together.

When we turned onto the Crieffs' street, Daniella perked up.

"Mom," she said, pointing toward a bus shelter. "That bag lady's back."

I straightened in the back seat of the car and looked outside. In the darkness I could just make out the form of a woman slumped over.

"Don't stare, Daniella," Mrs. Crieff said, her fingers tightening on the wheel.

"Why is she here all the time?" Daniella asked and shifted sideways in her seat. I turned my head, straining to see out the rear window. Something about the woman made me feel homesick. But for what? Toronto? Montreal? Dad?

"There are lots of people like that in Toronto," I said.

No one answered.

Before turning into the driveway, I looked across the street. In the glow of a streetlight, I saw the cream-coloured porch, the brown brick building that had once been my home. It looked different. The tree was gone. The driveway seemed shorter. Strangers lived there.

"It's hard to come back, isn't it?" Mrs. Crieff's voice was gentle. I nodded, longing for home. But I no longer knew where home was.

Chapter two

The smell of *tortière* greeted me as soon as I crossed the front stoop. *Tortière* was the fancy name for hamburger, chopped up with onion and served in a pie instead of a bun. It used to be my favourite meal when I lived in Montreal. Had Mrs. Crieff remembered?

"Well, hello stranger! Long time no see, kiddo."

"Hi, Mr. Crieff."

"Still Mr. Crieff, is it?"

"Yeah," I said, setting down the violin and sliding my backpack off my shoulder. "Thanks for having me."

"You're very welcome, *Ms. Chisholm*," Mr. Crieff teased and folded me into a bear hug. A few months after Mom died, the Crieffs had told me to call them Adèle and George.

I think it was their way of saying I could handle it — being a kid without a mom, I mean — that adults were still around who cared about me. I appreciated that, but the name change was offered too late. To me they'd always been Mr. and Mrs. Crieff and the titles stuck.

"Can we eat now?"

The voice came from the kitchen farther down the hall where Daniella's brother Kevin sat at a huge wooden table. He had a wedge of *tortière* in front of him and a fork balanced across the back of his hand.

"Hey, Marcie," he welcomed me, flipping the fork into his outstretched palm. "Can we have some of the *tortière,* Mom? The timer went off and the pie's ready."

"Wait a minute, Kevin. Marcie's our guest and I'm sure she's hungry, too, after the trip. Just give her a chance to wash up."

"Mom, he's so rude!" Daniella grinned and slid into a seat next to her brother. I washed my hands at the kitchen sink and sat down facing Kevin. He was my age — thirteen — and had been in my class once. He looked different. Older. His shoulders were broad and muscles had filled in his upper arms. A faint line over his lip marked the place for a moustache to grow. He was quite cute.

Kevin looked up and grinned.

Geeeez, I hate it when people hear my thoughts. Picking up my fork, I peeled back the crust of my *tortière* and waited as the steam flowed out.

"I asked George to put your bags in Daniella's room, Marcie," Mrs. Crieff told me. "You remember the way? Second door on the right at the top of the stairs. You'll share that room with Daniella."

I nodded and Daniella made a small sucking sound through the corner of her upturned lip.

"Well, I'll see you in a bit. I'm sure the three of you have a lot to talk about," Mrs. Crieff said on her way out of the kitchen. The three of us sat in total silence.

I watched Daniella scrape specks of piping hot meat from the tip of her fork to her front teeth. I couldn't believe how shy I felt. I used to love being at the Crieffs'. My "second home" Mom had called it.

When I moved to Toronto, I was so homesick for Montreal. I was nine years old and missed my room, my home, the Crieffs. More than anything, though, I missed Mom. "I can't believe I'm back here," I said.

"How long are you staying?" Daniella asked.

I was pretty sure she knew, but I told her anyway. Daniella glanced at Kevin and said something in French. I couldn't make out most of what she said, but I was pretty sure she was talking about me. Kevin shifted his eyes in my direction a few times.

Mrs. Crieff is Québécoise and teaches French at a girls' school downtown. She is completely bilingual and so are Daniella and Kevin. I haven't seen the Crieffs in four years, but that's one thing I still remember. When I was younger,

I thought Daniella and Kevin spoke in code. It seemed so unfair to me then. It still does.

My thoughts were interrupted by a snorting dog licking my leg.

"You still have D3?"

I had almost forgotten about the Crieffs' dog — a Boston bull with a nasal problem and a tongue too long for his mouth. I bent over and scratched his head.

"He doesn't like that," Daniella said.

Everything bugged her. She hated me. No question. I was off to a great start.

"Walk the dog, Kevin. He wants out."

"Uh-uh. It's your turn."

"Come on, Kevin, I had to go down to the station with Mom. Why should I do everything?"

"Uh-uh, I walked D3 last week."

"Thanks," Daniella mumbled, rocking the four legs of her chair as she stood.

Kevin laughed, scrubbed the rim of his plate with his index finger and sucked off the crumbs.

"Do you want me to come, Daniella?" I offered.

She raised one shoulder. "No, stay here. It's okay."

Kevin stood up, grinning.

"Poor you! All summer with Daniella," he said, then plunked his plate into the sink and picked up a cloth. "Don't you hate the smell of dishcloths?" he asked over his shoulder.

"Yeah," I agreed, though, to be honest, I had never thought about it before.

"Some people smell like dishcloths," Kevin continued. I wondered if I did — smelled like a dishcloth, that is. Slightly sour? A mixture of pickles and bleach?

I might have been wrong about Kevin. Taller maybe, but Kevin Crieff had not changed one bit!

Daniella's room had changed, though. The walls were ivory, now, but still covered in posters. A pattern swirled over the window blind. The same design was in a purple bedspread covering Daniella's bed, and on cushions thrown on the floor.

Beside the door, a huge soft-sculptured doll sat in a white wicker rocking chair. She had puffy cheeks and a jean hat pulled down over one eye. In her lap was a phone the exact shade as the bedspread. Everything in the room matched. Everything, that is, except one violin case and a canvas bag on top of my bed.

From deep in the chair, the purple phone rang. I can't explain why, but I knew it was Dad.

"Hello?"

"Hello, is that you, Marcie? I didn't expect you to answer. How's it going, honey?"

"Okay, I guess."

"What's wrong?"

"Nothing."

"Come on, what is it? What's the matter?"

"Nothing."

"You don't sound too happy."

"Mmm."

"How's Daniella?"

"She's okay. I guess."

"Good. Listen honey, you sound very tired to me. Give it a week and you'll feel right at home. You'll see. It's too early to tell. You just got there. Give it a chance. I'll let you go and call back in a few days. How does that sound, Marcie? Tell George and Adèle I say hello."

"Dad?"

"Uh-huh?"

I wanted to tell Dad how hard it was seeing our old house. How unfriendly Daniella was now. I wanted to beg Dad to come up and save me. "Oh, nothing. It's nothing," I said instead.

"Good. We'll talk next week, honey. Okay?"

I knew that we wouldn't. Dad might call, but we wouldn't talk. Not really. We never did.

"Okay," I said and hung up. Reaching across the bed, I flipped the bottom of my backpack and shook out my clothes. I was refolding t-shirts on my bed when Mrs. Crieff poked her head and shoulders into the room.

"Is everything okay in here, Marcie?"

"Yep, everything's fine. I'm just putting away my things."

Mrs. Crieff walked into the room and sat on the edge of my bed.

"I am so glad you finally decided to visit. I know it was hard for you to leave Montreal, and probably just as difficult to return, but we are really so pleased you are back. We were beginning to think you had dropped off the planet."

Mrs. Crieff smiled and cupped my face in her hands. I felt her rings gently pressing my cheek. Something about the way she was perched there made me think of my mother.

"I noticed you brought your violin," Mrs. Crieff continued. "Do you still compete?"

"No, not anymore."

I glanced at the spot under the bed where I'd already shoved my violin for the summer. Mrs. Crieff followed my gaze. A slight frown crossed her face.

"Well, maybe you'll play for us while you're here," she said. "I'd love to hear you again."

"Mmm-hmmm," I answered and carried a handful of shirts to the drawer. Dad must have put that idea into her head, but no way! I had loved to perform once. I could do things then. I used to be brave. Now, getting up in front of a crowd makes my whole body shake.

"My goodness, you are the picture of your mother, Marcie. There are so many things I want to talk to you about. It's been so long. But I know you are tired from travelling, so, for now, I'll just say goodnight. Daniella should be in shortly. Try not to stay up too late. You've had a big day."

I nodded and Mrs. Crieff quietly closed the door as she left.

I waited until I heard her shoes on the stairs then walked to Daniella's mirror. Searching my face, my eyes, I looked for my mother, but couldn't see her anywhere.

Mrs. Crieff was right about one thing, though. I really was tired. Slipping into my nightie, I walked to the window, plastering my face sideways against the cool glass. Through the branches of the oak tree, I saw the roof of the brown brick building across the street.

I turned off the light, kicked my sneakers under the bed and crawled in, pulling the covers close to my chin. I closed my eyes, still feeling the sway of the train, and seeing projected on my lids the form of a woman loitering in a bus shelter. Then, as sleep pulled me closer, I thought of the house across the street, and of a mother perched on the edge of my bed.

Chapter three

Daniella lay on her bed talking to me a bit. I was beginning to think Dad might have been right about getting along until I told Daniella the music I liked.

"They're no good," she said.

"I think they're pretty good . . ."

"No, Marcie, they're not."

"I like them," I said softly.

For some reason Daniella found this extremely funny. Rolling onto her side, she stretched her arm under her bed and pulled out her headphones. "You can't listen to that music in my room," she said, snapping the headphones in place.

How had I ever been friends with this kid? I couldn't figure her out. One moment she seemed okay, but moody or mean the next. Finally, I leaned back on my pillow watching the slow turn of the doorknob.

"Get out, Kevin," Daniella said without lifting her head. "Get out. I mean it."

The door opened and Kevin stepped in. He had one eye squinted shut, the other glued to a video camera. He focused on me, but I pulled my pillow in front of my face. That's all I needed!

"Get out. I'll tell Mom. Kevin, I mean it. GET OUT!"

Kevin spun around and panned the room with the camera while Daniella tilted her head and shrieked, "MOM!"

"Come down, now. Breakfast is ready," Kevin said, then backed out of the bedroom, filming my feet every step of the way.

At the mention of food, I smelled toast and realized how hungry I was. I pulled up the spread, and smoothed the top of my bed with my palm. Then I followed Kevin downstairs.

"Morning," Mr. Crieff said, swinging around in his chair. "How'd ya sleep, kiddo?"

"Fine."

"Where's Daniella, Marcie? Is she up?" Mrs. Crieff asked, loading bacon and scrambled eggs onto my plate. She spooned the same onto a plate for Daniella and motioned for me to pour juice.

"What's up?" Mr. Crieff asked Daniella as she strolled into the room behind me.

Mrs. Crieff looked at Daniella. "How are you, honey?"

Daniella didn't bother to answer. She sat down and scraped half her eggs and all her bacon onto Kevin's plate. She prodded the remaining eggs with her fork. "I'm not hungry."

"Well, how're you two getting along?" Mr. Crieff asked, but Mrs. Crieff interrupted before Daniella had a chance to speak.

"Marcie, there's a swimming program in the city this summer. No lessons or anything. It's strictly racing, but most of the kids around this area go. It's kind of fun." She took a sip of coffee and nodded toward her husband. "George's company sponsors one of the teams."

"Things have changed since you folks lived here," Mr. Crieff continued, the tines of his fork pointing toward me. "Back then, the city paid for all these things." He took another spoonful of eggs and crunched down on a corner of toast before speaking again. "Now, it's a different story."

"I was on Dad's team last year," Kevin said, wiping a line of juice with the back of his hand. He had a way of grinning that made his eyes crinkle.

"You were the worst on the team, Kevin," Daniella added.

"The kids would like to swim again this year, Marcie," Mrs. Crieff explained. "It's a big commitment, though. They're up very early every morning and the practices are three hours long. There's a race once a week and we all go and cheer. All the parents, I mean. Last year the local TV station even showed up to film the races a couple of times for the news."

Omigosh, she was going to ask me to go. Please, please don't ask me.

"Tryouts start next week," Mrs. Crieff went on. "We thought it might be nice for you to swim this summer, too. If you're interested."

I felt trapped.

Mr. Crieff took over then.

"Good way to meet kids, Marcie."

Bacon bits stuck at the back of my throat but I kept swallowing. How could I get out of this? I plastered a smile onto my face and looked from one Crieff to the next. Daniella held her cup mid-way between the table and her mouth. Everyone waited.

"Umm," I stammered. "May . . . maybe not this year."

Yeah, sure, maybe next year, or the one after, or in a decade or two. How many summers did you folks say you wanted me hanging around? "I don't mind going and watching you guys, though."

Kevin groaned and Daniella rolled her eyes so far back that it looked disgusting — like two hard-boiled eggs stuck into sockets.

"Nonsense! What fun's that?" Mr. Crieff asked.

"I really don't like swimming," I answered. It sounded pretty feeble.

"Oh," said Mrs. Crieff. I thought she looked disappointed,

but she smiled and passed the platter again. "Maybe you'll change your mind before next week," she said, patting the top of my hand.

"Yeah, right!" mumbled Daniella.

"Think it over, kiddo," Mr. Crieff chimed in. He turned sideways in his chair and snapped the newspaper. "Alouettes lost?" he grumbled. "I can't *believe* it. Look at this, Kevin. I was sure they would win."

Mr. Crieff glanced back at me, then, and switched to swimming again. "Not a big deal, Marcie. Just for fun. No one cares how good you are."

I nodded, trying to look as though I was already considering it. Truth is, how good I am has nothing to do with it. Sounds nuts, but I have this thing about people watching me perform. I don't really know why. It never used to bother me. Now, I get so nervous I think I'm going to have a heart attack. That's why I gave up violin competitions, can't give speeches at school anymore, and definitely will not join a swim team.

"What *do* you do?" asked Daniella. "In Toronto, I mean."

Why is it I can never think of anything to answer when someone asks that? I'm usually busy in Toronto, but doing what? I racked my brains for something. Anything!

"Dunno," I said with a shrug. *Good answer. Good answer.*

The boiled eggs appeared again.

"Well, I'm swimming," Daniella announced.

I really had to wonder why everyone put up with her. Dad

would take her attitude for about two seconds. I'd only been here a day, but it sure seemed to me that Daniella Crieff got away with a lot.

A strong odour of coffee and bacon hung in the air. My eyes wandered from the dish-piled sink to a row of eggshells on the stove. I heard the crunch of toast and the ting of forks against plates. Out of the blue I thought of the kitchen where my mother made waffles on Saturday mornings.

After breakfast I went upstairs, flopped on the bed and covered my face with my arms. Omigosh, there were fifty-five of these days to go. Fifty-five more breakfasts with Daniella, fifty-five more days without music, and fifty-five new excuses to come up with to avoid the pool. How would I ever make it through the summer?

D3 barked downstairs. A moment later, Daniella came in, slammed the bedroom door and everything was quiet.

"Daniella," I said before I lost my nerve. "Is it sharing the room? Is that what's bugging you?"

Daniella looked at me as though I had lost my mind, and I was just beginning to wonder if I had when she finally spoke. I think she tried to sound surprised, but I noticed her jaw tighten.

"Nooo. Well, okay, that's part of it. It's just, well . . . oh, never mind."

"If it's the room, maybe I could sleep on a couch some-where."

"Oh, sure! Like my Mom would let you sleep on a couch

somewhere." Daniella mimicked my tone. I glanced into the face that had once belonged to a friend and a stranger stared back.

"Sorry," I mumbled. "I just want you to know that I'm not trying to bug you."

"Look, Marcie, I'm fourteen years old, okay? I think I'm beyond being told what to do all summer. Or, who to spend it with. I've got my own friends. Besides, it's not fair for Mom and Dad to decide who is going to be in *my* room. That's exactly what happened. Your visit was planned like *that*." Daniella snapped her fingers in the space between us. "I didn't even get a say."

I felt a little closer to Daniella then. I'd been dreading my stay in Montreal, complaining to Dad about arranging my life. Not once had it occurred to me that someone else might be feeling the same. At last, I had found something in common with Daniella Crieff.

"No, you're right. It's not fair. And I know what you mean. It was Dad's idea. Not mine. Just like *that* it was all arranged."

I tried to snap my fingers the way Daniella had. No noise came out. Just then, a thought popped into my head and I wish to heck it never had. "Wait a minute," I said. "You're sharing your room with me, so I'll do something for you. I'll take over the job of D3."

I regretted it instantly, but it was too late. Daniella's head snapped up.

"Okay," she said. "He goes out a couple of times a day. I take him for one week and Kevin *supposedly* takes him the next."

I nodded, but Daniella wasn't finished.

"And swim," she said. "That's the least you could do."

What could I say? It occurred to me that Daniella and Dad might get along very well. "Maybe," I hedged. "I'll see."

Chapter four

Daniella covered her ears again with the headphones. Scooping magazines from under her bed, she sat cross-legged, flipping pages and tapping the side of her foot to a silent CD.

"Hello, ladies," someone called from the hall and a girl about my age walked into the bedroom. She had long red hair, a straight nose and no braces. I make a point of noticing things like that.

"Why are you cooped up in here?" she asked.

Daniella pulled off her headphones.

"Hey, Vickie. When'd you get back?"

The two talked while I sat like a lump on the spread until

Daniella finally waved a magazine toward me. "That's Marcie."

"Marcie Beaucoup?" the girl asked and giggled. Vickie obviously thought I wouldn't know enough French to get the joke. Actually, I didn't find mispronouncing *merci beaucoup* by mixing my name into it all that funny. I smiled anyway.

Vickie fixed her eyes on my mouth and I rubbed my tongue across my braces a few times. What had stuck in them now?

"When do you get them off?" Vickie asked.

"Not soon enough," I answered the line that kids with braces all know.

Vickie nodded. "I just got rid of mine this spring."

Anyone who has worn braces can't be all bad, I reasoned, and decided to give Vickie a chance. I would have, too, had Daniella not piped up.

"Marcie Beaucoup used to live in your house, Vic."

Over the next few days, I developed my plan. Daniella had always been a one-person friend so with Vickie in the picture, I was out. Every time Daniella ignored me, or Vickie — *Ms. Home-Snatcher-Ex-Braces* — came over, I had the perfect way to escape. Here's how it worked:

"Walk?" I'd say, jiggling the dog leash.

Wherever D3 was in the house, he would conveniently appear, nails clicking, chest heaving and we'd be out of there. Trouble with the system, though, sometimes, like *now*, I wasn't trying to escape. It was so early there was still dew on the ground!

D3 and I plodded down the street, stopping at every tree, shrub and plant. I'd discovered awhile ago that tugging the leash didn't faze D3. The dog stood firm, straining against the chain, rooting his legs to the ground like tent pegs.

"Come onnnn," I begged. But we slogged along, sniffing everything from house-to-bush-to-flower-to-tree.

When the Crieffs' driveway was finally in sight, I un-snapped the leash and headed inside.

D3 did not follow.

"D3," I screamed at the black and white streak racing across the road. He never looked back. D3 had more pep than I'd expected from an old dog. He scrambled toward the bus shelter, his stumpy legs spinning like one of those wind-up toys.

I heard D3 growl long before I'd caught up to him. What was wrong? He had never sounded like that before. "D3," I shouted. "Here, boy!"

There was a fake, cheery tone to my voice, but I was really afraid to approach the bus shelter. I slowed to a walk and clapped my hands together, making as much noise as I could. "Here, boy! C'mon D3!"

A raspy, chalk-on-a-blackboard voice cut through the early morning air.

"Git! Ga-wan, mutt!"

I moved toward the sound, taking baby steps along the grass.

"*Allez!*" the voice scraped.

At the bus shelter, I hung onto the edge of glass and peered around. A woman jostled back and forth across the shelter, trying to tear something from D3's grip. Her voice was sharp. I recognized her, although I'd seen her only once, slumped in this shelter the night I'd arrived.

The woman looked worse by daylight. She wore a grimy, too-large housedress and brown tie-up shoes. Nylons rolled over the tops. She yanked a worn canvas bag and kicked at D3.

Again I called the dog.

The woman's matted head snapped up. "Git yer dog," she snarled through blackened teeth. Her eyes were glassy. Wild looking. And she smelled of alcohol.

"Get off, D3! Let go!"

I heard hysteria bubbling up in my voice and forced it down several notches. "Here, boy!" I pleaded, trying to sound calmer. I patted my thigh.

D3 held fast to the woman's bag, a growl deep within his throat. I reached straight-armed and grabbed his collar. D3 didn't let go but shifted his eyes and growl toward me. His teeth were bared, his gums exposed. I gasped and jumped back, releasing the hold.

By swinging her bag, the woman managed to lift D3 right off the ground. His legs scrambled at air. He would not let go.

I pressed my back against the glass, trapped, afraid to grab the dog, but more afraid of the woman's twitching, widening eyes. Her head tilted backward, as though she might fall. Instead, she jerked her chin forward and spat on the floor near my sneaker.

I couldn't look. I raced around the bus shelter, hands over my nose and mouth, the stench of soiled clothes and alcohol making me gag.

I didn't see the cruiser at first. It crawled in beside the curb. When the siren beeped, I jumped and a piercing shriek — that I soon recognized as my own — tore through the glass enclosure.

My scream must have jolted the others as well. D3 lost his grip at the same time the woman lowered her wrist. The contents of her bag spewed across the shelter.

The officer spoke sharply.

"I, I d-don't speak F-french," I stammered.

For the first time since I'd arrived, I desperately wanted to be with Daniella. My imagination whirled in fast forward. Was I being arrested? Would the Crieffs find me? Tell Dad? My breath cleared my lungs in sharp, painful wheezes. In fact, D3 and I sounded a lot alike.

Nicotine-stained hands grabbed frantically at bits and pieces as the woman reclaimed her possessions. She stuffed the strange assortment — a blouse, a length of parcel cord, a couple of unmarked cans — into her ripped bag.

"You again, Renée?" the officer shouted. He held three fingers in front of the woman's face. "It's three times, now, that I have trouble with you."

He reached for the woman's elbow, but she yanked her arm out of his grasp.

"C'mon now," the officer said and clamped his opened hand on her forearm. He led the woman, head low, toward the waiting cruiser. Only once did she turn. She seemed puzzled. As though she had just noticed me.

I retreated quickly into the shelter, a turtle inside the safety of shell. When I peered out again, the woman was inside the car. The officer walked back toward me.

"That woman there. She's bothering you?"

"No," I screeched too loudly and cleared my voice. "N-no, it w-was the dog."

I pointed at D3. Omigosh! I was trying to blame the Crieffs' pet. "M-my f-fault," I stammered. "I let the dog g-go."

The officer stared at me. "Are you from around here?"

I bobbed my head, yes. Not a complete lie. I stared at the walkie-talkie attached to the officer's shoulder belt. I was so nervous, gulping back air, my heart pummelling my ribcage as though trying to break free.

That awful feeling of trying to remember something — something important — clawed at my brain. I felt dizzy and had to get away. But a memory snatched me out of the shelter and hurled me back four years. I remembered an older officer, standing over me, barking out questions. *You okay? You okay?*

It came back in fragments. Rapid shouts into a police radio. Short static snaps. Eyes staring. A crowd at the curb.

People yelling. Hands flying to mouths. Watching. Waiting.

I shook my head again and again until every shred of that awful memory erased. Somehow, I stuttered who I was and what I was doing on the streets at dawn with a dog.

D3 walked home without sniffing lawns. I was trying to stand up on spaghetti legs, my knees buckling every couple of steps.

"Problem?" Mrs. Crieff asked when I wobbled through the door.

I pointed an accusing finger at D3. "The d-dog . . ." I started, but stopped. D3 was in the hallway panting, wagging his tail-less bottom at me. What was the use?

"No, no problem," I lied.

Chapter five

Within the next week, I knew my way around the neighbourhood again, and had found a place where Mom used to buy ice cream. Inside the shop, I could almost imagine my mother still there.

It was hot, but I walked all the way to the metro before turning back. By the time I got to the Crieffs' house my toe was rubbing the inside of my sandal and rivers of chocolate ice cream ran down one arm.

Kevin sat on the front stoop, basketball twirling between his fingers. "'Bout time you got here," he called. I felt my stomach flip-flop. Had someone actually missed me?

"Your dad called."

"He did? Does he want me to call back?"

"No. He's on assignment. He says send an email. He'll phone again next week."

Kevin shot the ball toward me. I caught it in two sticky hands and one stomach, then crouched down on the step beside him.

"Don't forget tryouts are today," Kevin said.

"Kevin, I can't swim. I mean, I *can*. I know *how*. But, I'm too nervous to race."

"Come on. It's fun! Don't be such a wuss. You can do it."

Sure, sure, wipe out hunger, cure cancer, swim races. Hey! Why not solve the world's other problems while I'm at it?

"Besides," Kevin went on, "Mom said we were all going or nobody was."

Many excuses flashed through my head. I was choosing the best when I changed my mind. I'm not sure whether it was Kevin, making racing sound easy, or the thought of plunging my sweat-soaked body into a pool, but whatever it was, I heard myself say, "Okay, I'll go."

Dropping the basketball, I opened the door and went inside to cool off. I had agreed to go to the tryouts, but had also been careful not to actually say that I would try out. So, there was still a chance to back down.

Swinging around the banister, I climbed the stairs two at a time. Halfway to the landing, I heard music and knew Daniella was home.

Stacks of magazines, CDs and clothes blocked my path into the bedroom. The pile toppled when I pushed my weight against the door. I carefully squeezed into the room.

"Give me that!" I roared when I noticed Vickie, cross-legged on the floor. My violin lay sideways across her lap, ukulele style. I crunched something under my foot as I marched toward her.

"Okay, okay, don't take a panic," she said, holding the instrument up with one hand. I grabbed the violin, fighting the temptation to hit her with it.

"What's the big deal?" asked Daniella. "You never play it."

Daniella's comment lit small blow torches under my skin. "My mother bought me that," I snapped.

"So?"

"My mother's dead," I shouted. "Can't you understand?"

"You're still not over that?" Daniella asked. She made it sound like a flu I'd been unable to shake.

Vickie took one look at my face. "Gotta go," she said, smoothing creased shorts as she stood. "See you this afternoon, Daniella."

I clenched my fists as Vickie brushed past, expecting her usual crack about Marcie Beaucoup.

"Sorry," she whispered instead.

Daniella frowned and followed Vickie downstairs, leaving me alone in the room. I held my violin up to the rays that streamed through the window. Nothing had better be wrong.

Squinting my eyes, I scrutinized every inch of that instrument, front to back. I ran my palm over the surface of wood and checked each string with my thumb. Boy, did it ever need tuning! With my left hand clutching the neck, I swung the violin toward me, tucking the flat black plate under my chin. It was really too short for me now.

For the next while, I tuned and plucked and tightened the strings. I took a small clump of rosin from inside my case and slid it back and forth across the bow. Then I shut my eyes and played.

Not a lot. Scales mostly. Notes climbing and sliding, strings humming under the weight of the bow until, to my absolute amazement, my anger was gone.

"Sorry," I said when Daniella returned. "My violin is really special, I guess. I don't think I realized how much."

"No kidding!" Daniella replied.

About an hour later, Mrs. Crieff called from the bottom of the stairs. It was time to go. I gathered my towel and bathing suit and stuffed a change of clothing into my backpack.

"Do I need anything else?" I asked Daniella.

"Nah," she answered without looking up. Dipping the end of a cotton swab into a bottle of alcohol, Daniella puckered her lips and dabbed at her earlobes. "Ouch!" she said, turning her earrings.

"Kevin, do you know where my beach towel is?" she shouted.

Opening every drawer, she lifted out t-shirts and shorts and dumped everything onto the floor. "Seen my black towel, Marcie?"

"I haven't seen your towel," I said. "I'll check the bathroom, though. Maybe it's there."

Rifling through the hamper, I found the towel.

"The towel's wet and we're going, now, Daniella," I called through the door. Then I followed Kevin downstairs.

Mrs. Crieff was outside, unlocking the car.

"Would someone pop over for Vickie?" she asked Kevin and me.

Quickly, Kevin opened the car door. "I'm already buckled. Send Marcie."

I jumped in also and grabbed for my seatbelt. Not over there. Not to that house. No way!

Kevin stared at me. "Okay, I'll get her," he said.

Mrs. Crieff slid into the front and spoke into the rear-view mirror.

"You know, Marcie, it might not be a bad idea to go over there one day. I realize it's hard, but I don't think you can avoid the house, altogether."

"I know," I mumbled, watching Vickie come out of *my* house. She ran across the road and slid in beside me.

"Hey, Marcie," she said, dropping her bag onto the floor by my feet. "Thanks for the ride, Adèle."

Adèle?

Who gave Vickie the right to call Mrs. Crieff, Adèle? Her mother was alive!

Mrs. Crieff drummed both hands against the steering wheel. "Where is Daniella? She is keeping all of us waiting."

I expected Mrs. Crieff to turn the ignition and honk. That's what Dad does.

We waited.

After awhile Daniella strolled out. Mrs. Crieff shifted into reverse and backed down the driveway.

"Oops!" said Daniella, digging a hand into her swim bag. "Wait a minute, Mom. I forgot something." A frown wrinkled her forehead. "Please. I'll just be a sec'. I know exactly where it is."

Kevin, Vickie and I jerked backward when Mrs. Crieff braked, then forward, then back again. I was exhausted. Why had I worried about the tryouts? I'd be too old to swim by the time we got there.

The sun beat through my window, lighting small specks of dust on the glass. I narrowed my eyes against the glare. When we finally drove down the block, I peered out at the bus shelter. It was empty.

It occurred to me that Renée might have been arrested. I hoped not. I was the one who had let the dog off his chain after all. I looked up and down the sidewalk for a block or more. No sign of Renée. Did she have a home anywhere? A family? At least a friend who said when he saw her, *'Bout time you got here?*

The tryouts had already started when our tires crunched the gravel in the parking lot. Mrs. Crieff reached for her purse.

"I'll sign everyone up and pay, then you're on your own to get home, okay?"

"Yep," Kevin said. He and Daniella straggled behind. I know other kids who do that. As though they're embarrassed to be with a mother. I trotted along beside Mrs. Crieff, hoping someone would think she was mine.

Almost at once I saw Brad Dupuis. He'd been in my class every year since kindergarten. We'd taken music lessons together. Brad looked up and waved. I couldn't believe he remembered me. He'd always been popular, and judging from the crowd around him, he still was. I waved my fingers and Brad jogged over.

"Hi, Daniella," he said, draping one arm across her shoulder. He left it there while he talked to Vickie. Finally, Brad motioned to me. "Who's the new kid?"

"Marcie Beaucoup," Daniella chanted.

"Marcie Chisholm," I corrected. I'd had about enough of that joke. I didn't bother mentioning how long I'd known Brad.

"Get in the next tryout," Kevin whispered and the two of us headed toward the water. I still wasn't sure that I wanted to swim but wanted to hang around Brad even less.

I was standing ape-style, toes curled over the edge of the pool, fingertips clutching cement when the whistle blew.

Four swimmers straightened their legs and sprang forward, hitting the water with a loud clap.

Eight legs kicked, muscles tight, appearing and disappearing again and again in the frothy surf. Eight hands reached for the opposite edge of the pool.

I know because I stood ape-style, frozen with fear at the other end, watching them.

Chapter six

"Sorry," I mumbled and stooped over again, my fingers touching the edge of the pool, ready to actually dive in this time and swim. The whistle blew. I tried to spring forward into the water, but my toes wouldn't let go. It happened again. Then again.

"Look!" said one of the coaches, his deeply tanned face not far from mine. "Do you want to swim or not?"

I nodded.

"Then get in the darn pool this time or you're out."

I watched the muscles on his back ripple as he walked off. When he got to the far side of the pool, he spun on one heel, pointing his clipboard at me.

"I mean it!" he thundered. "This is your last chance. You're keeping all of us waiting."

I thought about Mrs. Crieff and the car ride over and wondered how long this guy would wait. I had the feeling I wouldn't get as long as Daniella. She was just plain spoiled.

I took my position again. My teeth were chattering and I hadn't even been in the water yet. Why on earth had I come? My throat seemed to be swelling. Maybe I'd choke to death and be done with it.

I don't know whose hand it was, but I definitely felt a gentle push. I hit the water full force — stomach, face, thighs. Everything stung.

Omigosh! I was drowning. Lifting my head above the surface, I gasped for air. The rest of my body thrashed and bobbed about like a beach ball. I had amazing energy. Panic must do that to a person.

With eyes tightly shut, I groped ahead, stiff-armed, legs kicking violently. It seemed so far. Sputtering, gasping, swimming a made-up stroke, I didn't quit until my forearm hit cement and my knee scraped along the bottom of the pool.

I jumped up and spun around, coughing and snorting water out my nose. The coach raised his clipboard and cheered. Daniella and Vickie were on the deck, mimicking my swimming technique, but I didn't care. Somehow, I had crossed the entire length of the pool and was standing knee-deep in the shallow end. I had actually done it.

It took another week before two teams were chosen.

"Daniella, Brad, Ajay, Vickie, and Chet are on the first team," shouted Andy — *Mr. Personality-Clipboard-Carrier.* "Here's your shirts. Don't lose 'em. We're lucky to have these sponsors."

Daniella held up the white and gold shirt to her chest and smiled. CRIEFF CONSTRUCTION was neatly printed in blue down one side.

"Oooh!" she said, as though she had no idea her father sponsored the team. Big surprise!

"Marc, Kevin, Rebecca, Tony, you're on the second team," Andy continued.

I clasped my hands together. Safe! I hadn't made either team.

Andy looked at me and snapped his fingers together. "Oh, yeah, and Marcie. You're on that team also."

Our team had black and orange shirts, the words LAKE-SHORE LUMBER splashed in block letters across the front. I stood by the side of the pool and glanced at my teammates. We looked like a pack of kids ready for Halloween. I shook my head. No question. The swim team would rival walks with D3 as one of the highlights of my summer.

"Now you can't all swim at the same time," Andy announced when we assembled at the deep end of the pool. "We saw last week that some swimmers are much stronger than others." He looked directly at me.

"I'll be working with Crieff Construction every morning. The rest of you see what you can do with Sammy over there." He pointed his clipboard toward a tall coach who had curly gray hair and glasses that rested high on his nose.

Raising a long thin arm in a wave, Sammy smiled as though our team was the one he had hoped for. As far as I could tell, Sammy had one huge advantage over Andy. He seemed human.

"Everyone in my team, please jump into the pool and swim down to the shallow end," Sammy called.

I sat at the edge of the pool with my feet dangling, inching myself forward. One of the boys on my team took off beside me.

"Cannonball!" he screamed, smacking the water with his curled up body. The splash drenched the rest of us.

"Hey, watch it, Tony," someone yelled.

Tony shook back his hair when he surfaced and swam to the ladder. He had amazing speed for our team. He took a breath, flipped over backwards and started down the length of the pool, pounding the water like a boxer.

"Cannonball!" Kevin shouted with Marc right behind.

Rebecca and I rolled our eyes. She dove and I slipped into the pool and followed.

"All right. Now try the width a few times while I watch everyone's stroke. We'll stay down here, out of the way of the other team," Sammy explained. "After today, we'll have the whole pool to ourselves every afternoon."

I squinted up at Sammy and smiled. The first team swam in the morning. If we practised every afternoon that meant

I wouldn't see Daniella all day. Sammy made a motion with his hand.

"Do your laps, Marcie. Back and forth. Off you go."

The other kids were heading toward me now. I took a deep breath but held my face out of the water. Wherever Kevin swam, I dog-paddled behind. "Don't leave me alone, okay, Kevin?"

"Why? Are you scared?" Kevin laughed and kicked away as hard as he could. Rebecca swam up beside me.

"It's okay. I'll swim with you," she said.

The two of us chugged across the pool and clung to the wall at the far side. We hung by outstretched fingertips, kicking our legs while everyone else swam back and forth.

"Is Kevin your brother?"

"No, he used to be my neighbour. I'm staying at his house for the summer. I live in Toronto now."

"Really? I just moved to Montreal a few weeks ago. I don't know anyone yet."

"Marcie, come out here a minute," Sammy interrupted. "We need to work a bit on your style."

Rebecca pushed off from the wall and joined the others. I hauled myself out of the pool and padded over to Sammy. The cement felt hot on my feet and I noticed a smell of chlorine on my skin.

"You can swim, right, Marcie?"

I nodded.

"Okay, then try this." Sammy positioned his opened palm

on my scalp. "Turn your head. Big breath. See that?"

I said that I did.

"As soon as you breathe, Marcie, your head turns and your face goes in the water."

I stood on the concrete inhaling, turning my face and stretching one hand, then the other high in the air above my head. After awhile, Sammy nodded.

"Now, you've got it, Marcie. Jump in and try that in the pool."

Compared to the deck, the water felt cool. I shivered and crouched down until my body disappeared up to my chin. Taking a breath, I pushed off. When my face hit the water, I opened my mouth.

Augh! Augh!

"Marcie, keep your mouth closed in the water," Sammy said. "Just the way you did up here. Go on and try again. I'll watch."

I took another breath and sealed my lips together. Reaching forward with one arm followed by the other, I actually started to glide across the pool.

"Watch out!"

I put my feet down and stood up, facing Marc.

"Sorry, Marc. I thought I was swimming in a straight line."

"Well, you're not! Keep your eyes opened!"

"Open? Doesn't that sting?"

"Not as much as a shoulder does when someone plows into it!"

"Okay, sorry," I apologized again.

I swam forward with my eyes opened, aware of legs underwater. The next lap felt shorter. I was actually picking up speed.

Four days later, we had our first race.

"Glad you're in there pitching, Marcie," Mr. Crieff said on the way to the pool. "Do your best. All anyone can ask."

"What's your team like, Daniella?" Kevin asked. He seemed almost excited to be racing.

"Great! A lot better than last year. At least everyone can swim!" Daniella didn't seem too interested in our team, but that didn't bother Kevin.

"Who're you racing?" he asked.

"West Island, I think. You?"

"Côte-St-Luc. They're supposed to be good."

Why didn't they stop talking about it. My stomach scurried around like a squirrel every time I thought about the race. By the time we parked the car I could hardly breathe.

Mr. and Mrs. Crieff waved to several people who were at the outdoor pool.

"This is our summer guest," Mrs. Crieff explained more times than I wanted to hear. Finally, the Crieffs snapped open their deck chairs and sat down. The place was packed. Swimmers wandered around everywhere, all wearing t-shirts bearing the name of a team. A lifeguard sat on a high tower overlooking the water and several clipboard-types strutted around with whistles.

I looked across the pool. At the far end, opposite the change rooms, I saw a table with three chairs around it. Andy and Sammy stood behind, draping large sheets of paper onto the surrounding fence. The words "Lakeshore Lumber" vaulted off one of the pages at me, and a tight knot formed in my throat.

What had I gotten myself into?

Chapter seven

Vickie walked toward us, scanning the crowd.

"Adèle, have you seen Mom?" she asked when she reached our chairs.

Not yet. Is she coming?"

"She *said* she would."

"Do your best, Vickie. Don't worry about your mom. She'll come," Mr. Crieff reassured her.

Vickie nodded. "Hi, Marcie. Good luck!" she said to me before wandering off to join Daniella.

"Do you really think she will show up, George?" Mrs. Crieff asked.

"Course not! Babs Porter has no time for swim meets."

I wondered why. I wanted to ask Mrs. Crieff but a popping sound caught my attention.

"*Mesdames et Messieurs, Garçons et . . . crackle, crackle. Bien . . . VENUE, excuuusse, bienvenue a . . . crackle.*"

Silence. Good Omen.

When the loudspeaker finally worked, someone announced that Crieff Construction would swim against a West Island team called Magnitude.

Daniella took her position first. She didn't even look nervous. She bent her long slender body, tanned hands gripping the side of the pool, and waited like a leopard eager to pounce.

Vickie stood behind. A hand shielded her eyes as she skimmed the crowd. Brad was next, stretching out his legs, performing semi-splits on the concrete. Ajay puffed up the muscles in his arms and grinned. Chet, the lucky one, stood at the end of the line.

At the pop of the pistol, Daniella dove into the water. Her long graceful arms glided across the water's surface as she propelled her body forward with powerful kicks.

Watching Daniella was like watching a fish in an aquarium. I couldn't take my eyes off her. At the far end, she ducked her head, disappearing under the water and flipped around. She resurfaced and started back, swimming toward us.

"Kevin," I said, clutching his arm and frantically shaking. "Both ways? Do we have to swim both ways?"

I should have known. We had practised turning all day yesterday.

"Yeah, both ways."

Kevin looked back toward the pool. He cupped both hands around his mouth. "C'mon, Dan," he yelled.

Mr. Crieff leapt up, pumping the air over his head with one fist. "Let's go, Daniella. Like you can now. Like you can."

Wherever I looked, people were cheering, arms waving. I heard clapping and shouting. The loudspeaker snapped on and off. People roared. Hands flew to mouths. The sun was hot on my scalp and my head ached. I looked across the sea of faces and a familiar sensation crept over me. I felt out of focus, as though I was supposed to do something — something important — but I didn't know what.

My heart roared into my ears and pounded my temples and wrists. Closing my eyes, I dug ten fingers into the sides of my head and waited. I had to get out of there.

I sprang to my feet, but so did Kevin. Ours was the next team to swim.

Stumbling toward the edge of the pool, I moved without feeling my feet on the pavement and took my place for the race. All I could see were eyes. Eyes waiting and watching and all staring at me.

The crowd blended into one huge face, opening its wide mouth and screaming.

Then the image blurred and small blue splotches floated in front of my eyes. The noise faded. Then there was no sound at all.

"I can't believe you fainted," Daniella said on the drive home. "I mean it's just a race. What's the big deal?"

"Enough, Daniella," Mr. Crieff warned. "Marcie feels bad enough."

"We all feel bad," Kevin said.

"Sorry," I murmured. My head buzzed and I rubbed the egg that was forming where I'd hit my head on the side of the pool when I fell.

TIMBER!

Try your best, Mr. Crieff had said when we'd started out. Let's see . . . panic, faint, disqualify my team. How am I doing so far?

Sammy phoned that night to see how I was feeling. I felt like going home. Where was that? I felt like choking Daniella. I felt like seeing Mom. "I feel fine, Sammy," I said.

"Don't blame yourself. Happens all the time."

"It does?" I asked. "Really, Sammy?"

"You bet. Teams are always getting disqualified for one reason or another. We should have had someone else ready to swim. Get some rest, Marcie. You'll feel better tomorrow."

When I hung up the phone I felt worse and went up to bed.

"If you feel dizzy or nauseated, Marcie, we'll call the doctor," Mrs. Crieff said as she folded a cold washcloth and placed it on the lump on my head.

Daniella was so lucky. And she didn't even realize it.

"It was your first race," Mrs. Crieff went on. "That's enough to make anyone nervous."

"I think I'm okay. It really wasn't the race. It was all those people shouting. And the heat and . . . and . . ."

Mrs. Crieff patted my hand. "I know, Marcie. I understand. I'll sit here with you for awhile. How's that?"

Sometime in the middle of the night, I woke and decided to call Dad. Riffling through my bag, I found the numbers he had scribbled down and tiptoed downstairs.

I didn't turn on the light, just quietly lifted the phone to my ear. Listening to the dial tone, I waited until my breathing had slowed, then pushed in numbers one-by-one. I had two more digits to press when the light clicked on.

"You wouldn't be calling your father by any chance, would you?"

I spun around quickly.

Mr. Crieff was in his pyjamas, a blue robe tied tightly around his waist. He lifted a golf club slightly. "Thought you were a burglar," he explained.

"Mr. Crieff," I started, replacing the receiver into its cradle. "Mr. Crieff, I can't stay here. It's too hard for me ... I ... I ..."

Mr. Crieff raised his hand to cut me off, then sat down on the bottom step. He motioned for me to do the same.

"Marcie, your life's been hard. No question. You were a young girl when your mom died. Too young. It was a tragedy. What's worse, you were there when she was hit by the car. Takes a long time to get over something like that."

He rubbed his hand through his hair. I widened my eyes until they hurt and stared at a vent in the hall. Everything looked blurry. Don't say anymore. Don't say anything more.

"But your mother's gone now, Marcie, and you have to

find a way, somehow, to get on with your own life. What happened at the pool today is not the end of the world. You're embarrassed. Big deal. What's one race, eh?"

I didn't answer and Mr. Crieff went on.

"A few weeks ago when I spoke to your father, he said how much he wanted you to come here. To try and work through all this. I'm not your father, Marcie, but this I know — if you leave here now, you will regret it later. Keep at it. Keep pitching. Don't be a quitter."

Search for your strength. Don't give up.

With the back of my fist, I wiped the tears that trickled down. Mr. Crieff looked at my face. He stood then.

"Think about it," he said. "You can stay, or you can go. Your choice, Marcie. If you want to stay — great! You know that you're welcome. We all want you here. But, if you want to leave, well, I guess that's okay, too. Call your dad and we'll arrange something."

Halfway up the stairs, Mr. Crieff leaned over the bannister. "Whatever you decide, do it with the light on, for heaven sakes."

What was he talking about? How could I leave? Where would I go? Mr. Crieff was beginning to sound like Dad.

I sat on those steps for hours. Thoughts chased each other around my mind. Search for your strength. Don't quit. Go home. Don't give up. Swim. You'll lose. Loser.

I had put in three weeks at the Crieffs' house. Three weeks out of eight wasn't that bad. Almost halfway home. And the practices were okay, I guess. But then at the race, I'd fainted, fallen in front of all those people. In front of my team-mates. How could I face them again?

Still, I had put in three weeks.

Three weeks with Daniella seemed like a year. Three weeks with D3. Three long, hard weeks.

But at least I'd done it.

I'd put in over twenty days. I'd walked that dog every day, except one. I'd promised Daniella that I would, and I had kept my word.

I had managed the length of a pool and joined a team.

That was pretty good.

I'd spent every night in a house across the street from my mother's home and I'd done it alone. No thanks to Dad.

Outside, the birds began to chirp. When the first gray light of morning filtered in through the den windows, I staggered upstairs to bed. I had made up my mind to stay. Between my header at the pool and being up most of the night, I guess I should have felt pretty rotten.

But I didn't.

I felt proud of myself.

Chapter eight

I slept all morning and most of the afternoon, finally waking up around three. The house was silent, except for toenails clicking through the hallway upstairs and the jingle of dog tags. My head felt like I'd had brain surgery during the night. When D3 barked I opened the bedroom door.

"Sorry boy. I just can't take you for a walk today."

With two fingers squeezed through D3's leather collar, I descended the stairs at a fast, bent-over trot. I didn't let go until we reached the backdoor and D3 raced into the yard. This message was written across the magnetic board on the fridge:

Gone out. Won't be long. Kevin and Dad at football game.
Check on Marcie. Don't leave her alone!
Mom

My head felt stuffed with cotton. It took a moment to realize that Mrs. Crieff had left the note for Daniella. Curling my fingers and clutching the inside of my pyjama sleeve, I wiped the board clean with my hand. Into the living room I staggered and flopped down on the couch to wait for D3.

The doorbell woke me. "Sorry D3," I muttered and ran to the door.

"Hi," Brad said.

Squinting into the sunlight, I blinked sleep out of my eyes.

"Brad? I thought you were the dog."

Brad shuffled from one foot to the other.

"Uhhh, not quite, Marcie. Daniella here?"

I woke up completely. Surely I hadn't said that aloud! I laughed then shook my head, glancing down quickly. Omigosh. I was still in the old-lady-pyjamas Mrs. Crieff had given me last night. I tried to jump behind the door, sticking my head out at Brad.

I hadn't brushed my hair for nearly two days and come to think of it, I hadn't brushed my teeth either. "She's not here," I said through slightly parted lips, then I rubbed my tongue along the braces.

Brad grinned. "Well, what're you doing?"

"Me? I, ah, just walking the dog. I mean, waiting for the

dog." Good grief! I really didn't know what I was doing.

Brad stared at me then arched his eyebrows. "You wanna hang out at the mall?"

"Me?" Omigosh. I couldn't believe what I was saying. Of course he was asking me. Who else? The dog? "Okay, sure," I stammered.

The trick, though, was to back away from the door without modelling splashy purple flowers on pink cotton pyjamas.

"Brad, I've got to shut the door for a minute. Can you wait there for me?"

"Sure."

The last thing I saw when I closed the door was the huge smirk on Brad's face. I galloped to the back door and let in D3 before darting upstairs to change.

When I caught sight of myself in Daniella's mirror, I nearly died. There was a huge green and black bruise on one side of my forehead and dark circles under one eye.

"Can I borrow some makeup?" I asked, opening Daniella's drawer.

"Oh, sure. Help yourself to anything you want. I'm always delighted to share," I answered, mimicking Daniella's voice. I felt a bit guilty digging into her makeup, but what the heck. I was desperate. Besides, she should never have left me alone.

Finally, I brushed the velvety texture of my braces back to metal, washed my face, smeared another thick layer of glop over my bruise and pulled my hair into a ponytail. Not exactly a huge improvement, but it would do.

Hurrying downstairs, I opened the door and saw Brad leaning against the railing.

"Okay, Brad, I'm ready."

The mall was a few blocks from the Crieffs' house. We wandered through a couple of sports shops then headed for the food court.

Brad and I lined up at a counter for Cokes. We were so close our shoulders touched and I smelled a combination of spicy cologne and chlorine. Brad's brown eyes stared at my bruise. "How's your head?"

"Oh, fine," I said as though I landed on my head every other day or so. I almost added, "How's yours?" but stopped myself just in time. I tried to think of something else to say but couldn't.

It occurred to me that Daniella would never have this problem. She didn't even bother with conversation half the time. It was up to everyone else to figure out her mood and act accordingly. Honestly! There was no justice in life.

"What time's your swim practice?" I finally managed.

Boy, what a conversationalist. I sounded like Mrs. Crieff. Next I'd be asking what grade he was in or if he had brothers and sisters.

"There isn't a practice, Marcie. It's Sunday."

"Oh, right."

"Cokes," Brad said, holding up two fingers.

The server lined up our drinks. We took our Cokes, leaving the plastic tray at the counter and found a table.

"So, you're from Montreal, huh?" Brad asked while stirring ice around with his straws. "Why'd you move to Toronto?"

"We moved when . . . when m-my mother died." I still had a hard time saying those two words together.

"Why?"

I shrugged and sipped my Coke. *Why?* How could he ask that? No wonder Brad and Daniella got along so well. He was as clueless as she was.

"Why?" Brad repeated. "What's your mom's dying got to do with it?"

"I don't know. It was easier for my dad to be somewhere else, I guess." I hoped Brad couldn't hear the wobble in my voice.

"You going to Vickie's party?" he asked after a moment.

Vickie's party? Vickie was having a party? How could I be living in Daniella's house and not know Vickie was having a party? Why hadn't Vickie invited me?

"When is it?"

"Friday. I thought you knew. Daniella said you did. She said you were thinking about going."

Thinking about it? What right did Daniella have to talk *for* me, she didn't even talk *to* me. But the truth was, I could hardly look at Vickie's house, let alone walk inside. Maybe Daniella sensed that and was thinking about my feelings.

Maybe that's why she hadn't mentioned anything. Nah! Not Daniella. It had to be something else.

The food court grew sort of quiet just then and I noticed the woman from the bus shelter. She shuffled around, eating scraps of burgers and fries, anything that had been left behind on the tables. Her face was a weird gray colour, almost purple, and her eyes were swollen and red.

"What's *she* doing here?" a woman sitting alone at the table behind us complained.

I'm not sure who she was asking. She didn't speak to anyone in particular, but her voice was loud enough for all of us to hear. I tried to look in another direction but — along with everyone else in the food court — couldn't stop staring at the bag lady.

Not once did Renée look up. She grabbed the thick jar from one table and poured sugar into a cup that she found. Her hand shook as she jerked her wrist back and forth to stir.

"Sorry, ma'am, you'll have to leave," a guard, hurrying into the food court said to Renée. "Go on now or I'll call the cops."

"That's security. He'll settle this," the woman behind us continued.

Before the guard settled a thing, though, another shopper stood up. He pulled a five dollar bill out of his hip pocket.

"Wait! Can't you see she's sick?" he said to the guard. "I'll get her something to eat. That woman is starving."

The guard held a hand in front of his chest like a shield and shook his head. "Not this time. We can't have people like this coming into the mall. It's bad for business."

The guard turned back to Renée, "Come on, let's go," he repeated, escorting her away from the table by her elbow. Renée made a twitching motion with her head. Her whole body tensed and her shoulders hunched forward. I'd seen that motion before and wondered if she might spit. Brad and I exchanged looks then got up.

"Do you think she'll be okay?" I asked when we'd pushed through the mall door onto the sidewalk. Brad shrugged. Part way down the block I spoke again. "Who is she anyway? I saw her at the bus shelter."

"Everyone's seen her, Marcie. She's always around here." Brad watched his shoes as he spoke.

"Do you think she'll be okay?" I repeated.

"How would I know?" Brad answered.

Chapter nine

Mrs. Crieff pressed the back of her hand gently against my forehead and made a *tsk* sound.

"Where have you been, young lady?"

"I feel fine, Mrs. Crieff."

"Marcie, you don't look a bit fine. You're our responsibility while you're here and we've been worried. George is out right now searching for you. Where were you? Why on earth didn't you leave a note?"

Why hadn't I? The Crieffs were big on notes. That was obvious.

"I'm sorry, Mrs. Crieff, I didn't mean to worry you."

"Where were you?"

"I was just down at the mall for a Coke."

"We have Cokes here for heaven sakes, Marcie. Now march straight up to bed."

I heard a snort behind Mrs. Crieff, looked up, and caught Kevin's expression. I wasn't sure whether he was laughing at me or his mom.

"Up," Mrs. Crieff said again.

I wasn't used to having anyone fuss like that. I guess I should have been flattered that someone cared enough, but I wasn't. Inside I felt squished, as though I'd outgrown myself. Everything felt tight and stuck to the skin.

"Really, I feel fine, Mrs. Crieff. I'm fine."

"Up!" Mrs. Crieff repeated, pointing toward the stairs.

I had heard her use that tone before with D3. I'm not sure what expression crossed my face, but without warning, Mrs. Crieff dropped her hand slightly and pulled me into a hug.

"Marcie, I'm sorry. I should have just waited until you were up, but I thought you would be all right for an hour or two. Daniella was here. When I got home, she'd gone off to Vickie's and you were nowhere around. Daniella is up in her room now. She's been grounded."

Buried in Mrs. Crieff's hug with my ear against her throat, I could hear and feel trembling in her voice. "I'm really sorry I didn't leave a note," I said when she released me and this time I meant it.

"I'm sort of on my own in Toronto and I'd forgotten about mothers worrying," I explained, then paused to suck in a big breath. Instead, a huge sob escaped.

"I guess I'd better go up, after all," I said. "I'm sorry. I don't know what's wrong with me." I felt like a fool and looked over to see if Kevin was laughing again. He wasn't. He planted a little punch on my arm and quietly left the room.

Upstairs, I found a pile of clean clothes neatly folded at the foot of my bed. Another thing I wasn't used to. I'd been sorting, washing and folding my own things for years. Daniella didn't even put hers away. A couple of weeks ago I thought Daniella was lucky. Today I wasn't so sure.

"Hi," I said.

"Hello."

"I'm sorry you got into trouble, Daniella."

"Yeah."

Daniella was sprawled out across her bed, arms folded under her head. She stared at the ceiling and didn't ask how I was or even where I was. I walked to the window. Flattening my face against the glass, I could almost see the bus shelter down the street.

"I saw that bag lady today."

Daniella lowered her gaze from the ceiling but didn't speak.

"She looked terrible," I continued. "She was drinking sugar water and eating scraps at the mall. A security guard told her to get her out, even though a man offered to pay. It was awful. She really looked bad. I'm afraid she's sick. Really sick. She looked almost dead."

"Everyone dies," Daniella mumbled.

Hair stood up on my forearms as goosebumps shivered their way down. What was it about Daniella's comment that bothered me so much? I'd seen many street people in Toronto and always hurried by, looking straight ahead. Was that as bad as not caring if they died?

"Listen, Marcie," Daniella said, turning onto one hip. "About today . . ."

Daniella looked at my face then down at her rings. When her chin lifted again, her expression had changed. "I don't see why I have to stay up here just because you wandered off."

"I don't either," I agreed and flopped down on my own bed. It was bad enough I had to be cooped up without having to share the cell with Daniella.

There was a knock at the door and Mrs. Crieff came in balancing a cup of tea. She had a flat box tucked under her other arm.

"Drink this, Marcie, you'll feel better."

I took the tea and propped myself up against my pillow.

"I saw the woman from the bus shelter, today. She looked terrible," I said, half-hoping Mrs. Crieff would rush over with a cup of tea for Renée.

"Yes, I'm sure she does. Poor soul. It's an awful way to live."

Mrs. Crieff sat down on the side of my bed, fingering the edges of the box. She made no mention of tea for Renée.

"Marcie, there's something I'd like to show you. Vickie's

mother brought all this over to me after they had moved into your house. They found these things at the back of a kitchen drawer. I phoned Toronto and spoke to your father at the time. He told me to toss them, that they weren't worth the postage it would cost to send. But, as you can see, I didn't."

"Ma, how long do I have to stay in here?" Daniella asked.

"What? Oh, you can go out now, I guess. Marcie seems to be okay."

That struck me as an odd comment. What if I hadn't been all right? What if I'd had an attack at the mall? What if I'd died? Poor Daniella would spend her teen years up in her room, listening to CDs, and wishing I'd never come to Montreal.

"Anyway, I thought that I'd just hang onto it all," Mrs. Crieff continued when Daniella had left the bedroom. "I didn't want to go against your dad's wishes, of course, but I couldn't help thinking that you might just want these things. They belonged to your mother, Marcie. And to be perfectly honest, although they have no monetary value, I'm quite sure she would have wanted you to have these little mementoes. I know I would, had you been my daughter."

Only a few items lay in the box, but I fingered each one. A small plastic container filled with my baby teeth. A page torn from a colouring book. A small black notebook, recipes scrawled in the familiar backhanded printing. A Christmas photo. The last one of Mom.

My fingertips gently traced the figure in the photo. White blouse, collar turned up. Oval locket embedded with flecks of red stone. Curly hair. For the first time, I saw what Mrs. Crieff had seen. The curve of Mom's head. Her smile. Up close she looked exactly like me.

After awhile, I placed all the items into the box and tucked it inside my backpack. Mrs. Crieff was right. These were some of the things Mom had treasured. These were the things she had kept. Now they were mine. Sliding the pack under my bed, I took out my violin and unsnapped the case. My mother had been proud of the way I had played. I spent the rest of the afternoon practising scales until each note sounded right.

Later that night Dad phoned.

"Dad, Mrs. Crieff saved some of Mom's stuff for me."

"Really? That was thoughtful. What stuff?"

"Little things. A picture. Recipes. Even some of my baby teeth."

"Great. Things are going okay then? You sound pretty happy tonight."

"Yeah. Things are all right. Dad, there was a picture there of Mom. She looked like me."

"Yes, I guess she did a bit. What else is going on?"

"Nothing much. Dad, didn't you want to save those things?"

"What things? Oh, those. Well, I guess they didn't seem important at the time. It's not a big deal, Marcie, is it? Can we talk about it another time?"

"Uh-huh," I said. Before I hung up I mentioned that I had been picked for a swim team.

"Marcie, that is wonderful news. I am really pleased. I knew it would be good for you to go back to Montreal and try to sort things out for yourself. A swim team. That is just great."

It was true. I had been picked. I didn't bother telling Dad I had since decided to quit.

I spent the next few days hiding out or "recouping" as Mrs. Crieff generously put it. Most of the time was pretty boring, but there were some perks. I didn't walk D3 and I didn't have to swim. By Wednesday, though, even that had worn pretty thin.

I was downstairs in the family room when I noticed Kevin watching me. He came in and flopped into a huge armchair.

"You swimming again?" he asked.

"Not sure," I said, pointing the remote and clicking the power button.

"Marc's in the Laurentians. We don't have enough kids for the race."

Kevin sat there looking at me. When I didn't respond he continued, "Sammy wondered if, maybe, you would come back and swim the relay. It would only be one lap."

"Hmmm. I'd like to, Kevin, I really would, but I'm recouping." I had a hard time keeping the irony out of my voice. I'd missed the kids at practice but was in no hurry to race again. Again? I hadn't even raced the first time.

"C'mon, Marcie. There's not a thing wrong with you."

"Well, thank you, Dr. Crieff, for the free medical opinion. And, by the way, there's not a thing wrong with you, either."

I had meant it as a joke, but heard the strange catch in my voice. What was it about Kevin that made me feel that way? Embarrassed, sort of, and, well . . . nervous.

Kevin stood up. "Think about it, okay?" He didn't wait for an answer.

I picked up a pen from the desk beside my chair and wrote *Kevin Crieff* in big loopy letters across the TV guide. Then I scribbled it out so many times I made a hole in the paper. What was I thinking!

Chapter ten

I had wondered about Renée ever since Sunday, but it was the first time I'd been out of the house all week. The sun felt warm on my face and neck as I ran around the hedge at the side of the house and cut across the Crieffs' lawn.

When D3 and I arrived at the bus shelter, I slowed my step and shortened the dog's chain by wrapping it several times around my wrist. My heart was pounding and I looked over my shoulder, not sure I was doing the right thing. But the image of Renée scrounging for food had haunted me for days.

The bus shelter was empty. A couple of bottles scattered under the wooden bench made me think Renée had been back since the day at the mall. So I ducked into the glass structure and dropped a bag onto the bench. I'd packed the lunch quickly that morning — an apple, a bagel, cheese and a huge chunk of roast beef.

Before heading home, D3 and I circled the whole block. When I walked into the house, I heard Mrs. Crieff and Daniella in the kitchen.

"Daniella, she's not going to go into her old house, so forget it! It would be one thing if you had asked days ago. Given her a chance to think it over. But you chose not to, for whatever reason, and now it's too late."

I closed the door with a slight bang, rattling D3's chain. "I'm home."

It was Thursday and I was pretty sure Mrs. Crieff and Daniella were discussing Vickie's party, the one Brad had told me about. Brad, but nobody else.

I heard Daniella whisper something in French then Mrs. Crieff called out, "In here, Marcie."

I pulled a glass out of the cupboard and filled it with ice water for myself. Then I took D3's bowl from the mat and filled it with tap water. D3 lapped it up noisily. I stifled a sudden urge to laugh at his manners.

"Vickie's having a party. Did I tell you?" Daniella asked quickly when D3 had finished.

"No, I don't think you did."

"It's tomorrow night. Wanna go?"

"Umm, I'm not sure just now, Daniella. Can I let you know later?" I asked.

Daniella arched her eyebrows and shot a smug smile at her mother then spun her legs around the chair and faced me.

"Vickie's sleeping over tonight. Can you tell her then?"

I was going to say no, but Kevin walked in before I could answer.

"Don't you have swimming, Daniella?" he asked, opening the refrigerator and leaning against the door.

"Yep. I'm just going. Mom, can you drive?" Daniella grabbed her towel off the table and snapped it at Kevin. "By the way, Vickie and I think you should invite Rebecca to the party, Kev."

"No way!"

"Can you drive, Mom?"

The phone rang just as Mrs. Crieff picked up her keys.

"For you, Marcie," she called.

I reached for the phone, half-expecting to hear Sammy's voice. I braced myself. I had no intention of ever returning to practice and the sooner he knew it the better.

"Hello?"

"Hi, Marcie. This is Rebecca. Rebecca from the pool?"

She was the last person I had expected. Rebecca from the pool was exactly who Daniella was just talking about. Rebecca from the pool must have ESP!

"I was just wondering how you were, Marcie. You haven't been at the pool for ages."

"Oh! Umm, no, I haven't been there for awhile. I'm fine,

though," I laughed. "Thanks, Rebecca. I guess I really did a number at the race the other day, eh?"

"Yeah, well, at least you're okay."

"Yeah, I am. Thanks again for calling," I said, eager to get off the phone before she said anything more about the pool.

"Ahh, Marcie, I was just wondering if Kevin was around?"

Kevin? Why did she want Kevin? I thought about Daniella's comment.

"Just a moment, I'll see."

I held my hand over the phone while I took baby steps around in a semi-circle. "No, Rebecca, I don't see him around."

I can't explain why I didn't want Rebecca and Kevin to be at the practice together. But that afternoon I returned to the pool.

Tony was the first to see me. He sat by the side of the pool, wrapped in a beach towel. His lips were blue and quivered slightly.

"Think you can stay on your feet this time, Marcie?"

I stared at Tony. What a welcome!

"Yep, I think I can," I finally answered. "Might be a bit difficult, though, running along the bottom of the pool in the deep end!"

"Funny girl! Funny girl!" Tony said and swatted my shin with the corner of his towel. Sammy smiled and walked over to us.

"Marcie, I've thought a lot about what happened at that race. Don't feel bad about it. As I told you the other night on the phone, you're not the only one who has fainted. Many athletes get nervous the day of competition. What you've got to do is forget the crowds. Tomorrow the only race you have to swim is the relay. That's just one straight length of the pool. I know you can handle it. Are you up to it?"

"I think so, Sammy."

"That's the spirit! Now what you need is to keep your mind off the race. Try swimming second, right after Kevin. Watch him. Don't take your eyes off him. Stay focused. Visualize yourself diving, okay? As soon as you see Kevin's hand touch the wall — in you go. Don't even look at the crowds. Just imagine you're at practice."

"I think I can do that, Sammy," I said, not totally convinced that I could.

"Keep your eyes on Kevin," Sammy repeated.

We swam laps for the rest of the practice. Kevin and I raced against each other. We tried a couple of loops in our relay order while Sammy timed us. I watched Kevin's head as he swam toward me and tried to dive as soon as his fingers reached out of the pool. The trick was for me to take off, but not actually hit water until Kevin's hand touched the wall.

By late in the afternoon, we looked pretty good. I had figured out how to grip the cement edge of the pool with my toes and when to push off with my legs. I was diving in without thinking about it, and noticed that I wasn't gasping for breath anymore. Even my arms felt stronger. It now only took two tries to haul myself out of the pool.

"You're ready," Sammy said pointing at me. The kids cheered. None of them mentioned the first race. Maybe it really didn't matter to any of them.

Before leaving that afternoon, Rebecca opened her bag, took out a can of tuna and dropped it into a plastic tub beside the girls' change room. I was outside waiting for Kevin. Until then, I hadn't noticed the tub.

"Did you hear about this, Marcie?" Rebecca asked. She pointed to a sign on the bulletin board. I squinted my eyes against the sun and read, *Swim Race = Food Race!*

A handful of printed sheets stuck out of a cardboard slot beside the sign. I took one and folded it into my pocket.

"Did you bring food for that bucket?" I asked Kevin when he finally appeared at the door of the boys' change room. Kevin glanced at the bucket.

"No, I forgot. Sammy brought it last week. It's a food drive. All the teams make donations for Sun Youth. The team that collects the most by the end of the season wins something."

"What's Sun Youth?"

"Oh, it's an organization that gives food to people. Sammy said it was started years ago by a group of Montreal kids. Sun Youth runs sports programs too. That's our connection. Sammy said it would be good to help other kids have a chance to swim, or whatever they do."

"It's a good idea. I saw that woman from the bus shelter the day I went up to the mall. She looked horrible, gray, sort of. Some man said she was starving. Brad and I left after that."

Kevin stopped walking. "You went with Brad?"

"Yeah. The day after my accident. He came for Daniella, but she was out."

Kevin didn't say anything and I trudged along beside him until we were nearly home.

"I like the idea of a food drive a lot. I've felt guilty ever since I saw that woman at the food court. She was eating bits of food and gulping sugar water. I'll tell you something, Kevin, if you promise not to laugh."

"What?"

"D3 got into a fight with that woman early one morning. It was bad. He was growling, tearing at her things. I couldn't get him off. The police came and took her away. Renée is her name."

That was all I planned to tell Kevin, but he kept looking down into my face. He was really listening.

"I hate it when the police come," I continued hoarsely. The sound of my voice was eerie. I listened to myself as though hearing someone else speak.

"I hate the noise of those walkie-talkies. Hollow and snapping like the loudspeaker at the races. I hate when people scream. I hate when they watch me, expecting me to do something. Something important and I don't know what it is. I hate . . . I hate . . . Oh, Kevin, I hate that my mother died," I whispered.

I'd never said those words aloud to anyone before and I felt light, almost giddy. I wasn't sure whether I wanted to laugh or cry. I watched my sandals stepping over the lines of concrete. *Step on a line, you'll break your mother's spine. Step on a crack, you'll break her back.*

The side of Kevin's hand brushed against mine and I felt the squeeze of my fingers, wrapped inside his.

"I remember your mom," Kevin said. "I liked her."

Chapter eleven

"Brad swimming," Daniella yelled.

She held her arms over her head and took a running dive onto the bed. Kicking her legs in quick, jerky movements, Daniella rolled from side-to-side, turning her face up and gulping for air every three strokes. It reminded me of a video played on fast forward.

"Andy swimming," Vickie said when Daniella's imitation of Brad was over. She took a flying leap onto the bed, flipped to her back and shouted. "You kids're darn lucky to have me for a coach. Darn lucky!"

I bounced on my own bed. "Marcie swimming," I yelled and fell face-first onto the mattress, my whole body rigid, my hands plastered down by my sides.

"What happened to you that day, anyhow?" Vickie asked.

"Sammy told me to change my style. Think I went a bit overboard?" Vickie laughed and Daniella sang, "Sammy the wonder coach."

"He really is nice. I am so glad he's my coach and not Andy."

Vickie picked up a handful of potato chips, shoved them into her mouth, then passed the bag to me. "Are you coming to the party?" she asked.

"I'm not sure yet."

I reached into the bag and pulled out a couple of chips, wiping my salty fingertips off on Vickie's sleeping bag. I quickly slipped a chip into my mouth then tossed another high in the air. Opening my lips, I stuck out my tongue. "Caught it!"

"Yeah, sure. I saw the chip fall by your bed. There! There it is." Daniella pointed to a shape on the rug with the toe of her sandal. "You didn't catch it. You already had one in your mouth."

"Come to the party, Marcie. It's my thirteenth birthday."

"Really?" I knew Daniella was a year older than Kevin and I, so had just assumed that Vickie was fourteen as well.

"I wanted to ask you sooner, but didn't know how you'd feel about being at my house."

"I don't know either," I admitted.

Daniella shrugged. "Just go! It's no big deal. Leave early if you want."

"Yeah, you can do that," Vickie agreed.

"I'll probably go," I said.

Vickie had come for the night and the three of us were having fun. Even Daniella and I were getting along. Almost like the old days when we had been friends. I was finally beginning to remember what I had liked about her and how much fun she could be.

"Does my house remind you of your mom?" Vickie asked.

"Everything reminds me of my mom."

"It must be awful when one of your parents dies, eh? If I were you, I'd never have come back here. Never."

"Yeah, well, I didn't want to at first. Dad gets these big ideas. He never asks how I feel about anything. Now that I'm here, though, it's really no worse than being in Toronto. Although, I still don't know about actually going into my house. Or, I should say *your* house. I think that might still be too sad for me. I'm not sure. One thing I am sure about, though — Montreal really doesn't feel like my home anymore. Nowhere does!"

"At least your mom's dead," Vickie said, then quickly added, "I mean, at least you know she *can't* be with you, not that she just doesn't *want* to be."

I remembered Mr. Crieff's comment at the pool.

"Where's your dad?" I asked.

"He lives in an apartment north of here. In Laval. My Dad's okay. He's remarried and has a new baby. I don't see him often."

We all munched on chips for awhile until Daniella spoke.

"I know what you mean about not knowing where you belong, Marcie."

Vickie and I turned to Daniella then faced each other and rolled our eyes.

"How would you know?" Vickie asked.

"What do you mean? Of course I know!" Daniella answered.

"How?" I demanded. Ever since the night I arrived, I'd witnessed first-hand how the Crieff household revolved around Daniella. It was the same at the pool. How could she possibly know what it was like not to belong?

"Well, you know. I feel English around Québécois and French when I'm around English."

I thought about how envious I'd been that Daniella spoke both languages. It was unbelievable that anyone so popular would feel anything other than great. Maybe no one really felt that they fit in exactly.

"Never thought of that," Vickie said, scrunching the chip bag.

"Don't you think Kevin should invite Rebecca to my party, Marcie? She really likes him."

"Umm," I said. I felt my face warm up. This was really getting bad.

"He won't ask her," Daniella said, and I actually felt relieved.

"Know what I did today?" I asked. I hadn't planned on

telling anyone, but wanted to talk about something else. "I packed a lunch and brought it over to Renée."

Daniella wrinkled her forehead.

"Renée? Who the heck is Renée?"

"You know, that woman from the bus shelter."

"Marcie, are you nuts?"

"You brought lunch to the bag lady?" Vickie hooted.

"I saw her the other day. After the swim race. She looked awful, like she was dying or something. Anyway, I felt, well, I wanted to do something."

"Wanna really help?" Vickie asked. She pulled her knapsack onto her lap, unzipped the front pouch and rifled though the bag until she found a crumpled flyer.

"Look at this," she said, flattening the paper. "It's a talent contest at the arena. We can enter."

"Vickie, get real!"

"No, seriously, why not, Daniella?"

"We have no talent."

"Maybe no one would notice," Vickie said with a laugh. "Besides, Marcie has talent. She plays the violin. And I can sing — a bit."

"Oh, right. And I'll be your manager," Daniella added sarcastically.

"Check this," Vickie said, spreading the folds out of the flyer and holding it up to Daniella. "If we win, we get $1,000 donated to our favourite charity. We could give it to Renée."

"Don't be ridiculous, Vickie. You're beginning to sound

like Marcie. Renée's not a registered charity."

"Nooo," I agreed with Daniella. "But there must be some way to do it. Some program for the hungry that *is* official."

"There's Sun Youth," Vickie continued. "They're the ones we collect for at the pool. Let's get Brad in on it. He plays, too. We could be a rap group."

"Rap on a violin? I don't think so," I said.

"What would we call ourselves?" Vickie asked, ignoring my comment.

"BAD. Call yourselves BAD before everyone else does," Daniella suggested.

We filled in Vickie's form using the name BAD and listing Brad Dupuis as the lead violinist, Dan Crieff as our group manager, and Sun Youth as our chosen charity.

The next morning, we ripped the registration form into tiny pieces and threw them around the room like confetti.

"Let's go eat," Daniella said and we headed downstairs.

From the landing, I heard Mr. Crieff in the hallway below.

"They just called me, Kevin. Broke in through the warehouse door. C'mon down, son, gimme a hand securing the place."

"Who did?" Daniella asked, swinging around the banister.

"Couple kids. Broke into that old warehouse near the refineries. Time to take that building down. No one uses it anymore. The thing is nothing but trouble."

Kevin looked at me, "There was a break-in at Dad's warehouse in the east end. We're going down there. Wanna come, Marcie?"

"Sure."

Daniella and Vickie gawked as though I had lost my mind. Then Vickie's eyebrows shot up and Daniella smirked.

"Bye-bye, Kevin," she sang.

As I closed the front door, I heard Vickie chime in, "Rotsa Ruck, Rebecca."

Chapter twelve

I never realized before just how long Sherbrooke Street was. According to Mr. Crieff, it stretched across the whole island, from Montreal West to the eastern tip of the city. Some of the three-storey homes we passed along the way to the warehouse looked really old with black lacy railings spiralling upward across the front.

"There's the Big O, Marcie," Mr. Crieff said. He pointed toward a structure that looked like a cross between a spaceship and a whale. "That stadium was built years ago for the Olympics. Still isn't finished. Would've been done long ago, if we'd had the contract. Didn't get the job, unfortunately, but we did build a lot of the hotels you see around here."

Turning south off Sherbrooke, we bumped over a level

railroad crossing and drove down a short street to the warehouse, a red brick building with ten large sectioned windows, mostly broken, or covered with dust and cobwebs.

Black and purple paint was splashed along the walkway and high on one wall. Over another, someone had spray-painted heavy black letters.

Mr. Crieff scowled. "What a mess!"

Parking close to the building, he shut off the engine and climbed out of the car. Kevin followed.

"I'm going to wait here, Kevin," I said. Unbuckling my seatbelt, I looked out at the abandoned oil refineries that stood in a weed jungle across the street.

Igloos with the tops cut off. That's what they looked like. Each with its own rusted stairway wrapped around a huge concrete belly. The place was the perfect setting for a murder mystery.

I locked the car door, slumping down low to wait.

After awhile, Kevin and Mr. Crieff came out of the warehouse and replaced the lock at the main entrance. When they were done, the three of us drove down the block to a small coffee shop.

There were a few customers at the far end of the restaurant, smoking. We chose a booth near the front.

Outside our window was another refinery. This one surrounded by monkey bars. That's what they looked like to me anyway. It was not quite as round as the ones I had seen near the warehouse. And not quite as scary.

"Does that thing still work?" Kevin asked.

"You bet! Look at the flame. They're stockpiling now. Saving up to heat the city this winter. In the spring, they'll refine oil here. Year-round business."

"Smells," Kevin said wrinkling his nose. "So did that warehouse, eh, Dad?"

"Glad to get that thing locked up. Can't have kids going inside. It's too dangerous. I'll get a better alarm installed. Don't know what else to do with it for now."

"My father said some group in Toronto was turning old warehouses into homes for the homeless. Places like yours, Mr. Crieff."

Mr. Crieff snorted and shook his head. He dumped sugar into his coffee straight from the jar.

"People live in a warehouse? Do they have rooms?" Kevin asked.

"Yeah. I think so. It's better than having the building vacant. It helps the homeless, too."

"Nothing but a band-aid treatment. Those people need work, Marcie. Not handouts," Mr. Crieff said.

I pictured Renée in her grimy housedress, thick sausage of nylon around her ankles, heading out for job interviews. "Wouldn't it be hard to get work without an address?" I asked.

Mr. Crieff snorted again and crunched into his bagel.

"Maybe we should try that, Dad," Kevin said.

"Eat your bagel, son."

"But there are lots of homeless people around, Mr. Crieff.

It's the same in Toronto. They have nowhere else to live. No work, no . . ."

"Enough!" Mr. Crieff replied, holding his palm up in front of me. "People can find work if they try."

I was surprised. Dad rarely agreed with anything I said, but he never cut me off like that. I dug my fingers into a rip in the red plastic seat and pulled out a bit of wadding. "I just mean people need to help each other, I think, I . . ."

"You're exactly like your mom, Marcie," Mr. Crieff said, not unkindly, but he had cut me off again. "You not only look like her, you think like her. Can't fix all the world's problems, kiddo."

"No, but we could do a couple of things," Kevin said.

"Kevin, please, one bleeding heart around here is enough." He tried to make it sound as though he was kidding, but I knew he was not. I had never seen this side of Mr. Crieff before.

"Nothing much you or I can do about the hungry or the homeless. People gotta help themselves," he continued.

"I think we can help a little. I brought roast beef to Renée a few days ago."

I felt Kevin kick my shoe under the table, but it was too late. Mr. Crieff put down his coffee cup and stared at me for several seconds.

"You what?"

"A bit of roast beef. To the woman who lives in the bus shelter. You know. The shelter down the street from us."

"You had no right doing that."

Mr. Crieff looked over his shoulder to the customers at the back. He waited several moments before he spoke again.

"Marcie, forgive me, I didn't mean to yell, but you have no business hanging around that bus shelter at all, let alone bringing food over there. It's not safe."

He looked then at Kevin. "What do you know about this?"

"Nothing. It was my idea," I said before Kevin could answer.

"Marcie, we pay taxes. We give money to the government. *They* feed the hungry. *We* do not. Y'a got that? Why're you doing this? Are you a social worker? Course not! You're a thirteen-year-old kid. It's not your job to feed the homeless. Good grief, you'll have every street person in the city at our backdoor looking for handouts. You had no business doing that. You don't even live here, for heaven sakes. You're only a guest at my house."

Welcome, welcome. Your home away from home.

"Dad!"

A red patch formed on Kevin's neck and crawled up toward his cheeks. "Lighten up. Marcie didn't do anything."

"Marcie knows how I feel," Mr. Crieff said. "No big deal. Just don't do it again, okay? No more dinners delivered to a bus shelter."

Mr. Crieff looked tired, dark circles outlining his eyes. He rubbed his hand through his hair and sighed.

"There is a food drive at the pool," I said meekly. I

sounded about five years old. "Kevin said it's for Sun Youth."

"Fine, fine. Bring something to that. Okay? You kids ready?"

Mr. Crieff stood then, picked up the bill and walked to the counter to pay.

"What the heck is his problem?" Kevin said. "I'm sorry, Marcie. He gets so worked up about nothing at times."

"Don't worry, Kevin. It's not your fault. You should see my Dad sometimes." I rolled my eyes, but the truth was, I couldn't think of a single time when Dad had sounded so upset about nothing.

The drive back was endless. Everyone talked about nothing for a few blocks. And then not at all until we got home.

That afternoon Vickie phoned to say her mom was swamped at work and the party was off for a couple of weeks.

"Her mom lets her down, doesn't she?" I said when Daniella told me.

"No kidding!" Daniella grumbled. Flipping her bangs back from her eyes, Daniella plunked on her headphones and sat with her back to the wall. "There goes the weekend!"

BAD and the sleepover seemed light years away.

Chapter thirteen

The race was at a pool in a new subdivision. The water looked a paler blue, cleaner somehow than the older pools. Further back this time, parents sat on bleachers overlooking the shallow end. There were no deck chairs. Across the pool, swimmers waited on a narrow strip of grass.

I scanned the racing list. Lakeshore Lumber was the first team to compete.

Good! Let's just get this over with. I had six or seven species of butterfly inside my stomach, but I was determined to race. Sounds crazy but, in my own mind, being able to complete a race had something to do with Renée.

Girl swims. Saves homeless.

I stood in position at the edge of the pool, waiting for the relay race to begin. Not once did I look at the spectators. I concentrated on the shimmering black lines painted onto the bottom of the pool. The sway of the water was hypnotic. I felt sleepy, almost in a trance when the pistol sounded.

"Get ready, Marcie," Tony whispered and I felt a soft tap on my back.

At the opposite end, Kevin splashed into the water, froth churning behind with each kick. I focused on the top of his head and the movement of his shoulders as he sped down the lane toward me.

We were racing a team from NDG and their lead swimmer was half a lap ahead of Kevin. She moved with powerful strokes. The moment she reached our side, her teammate contacted the water with a resounding splash. I gripped the side of the pool with my toes and waited to dive. Waiting and watching for Kevin's hand to touch the cement.

As soon as the tips of his fingers stretched forward, I sailed through the air and hit the water kicking. The shock of cold water energized my whole body. I turned my head upward for breath and saw my competitor ahead. The opposite end seemed a long way off.

Kick for Renée, I reminded myself.

Kick for Renée, I repeated over and over in time with my strokes.

Lakeshore Lumber didn't win that race. We didn't even place, but I didn't care. I had completed my lap.

"We should have come first today," Daniella said on the way home. "We could have, too. We should have been faster. Ajay was slow diving in, eh, Dad?"

"You were fine, Daniella. The same team can't win every race," Mrs. Crieff pointed out. "Crieff Construction placed second. That's good enough."

"Your mom's right. The same team can't always win. A little competition is good," Mr. Crieff said, then added, "Ajay wasn't paying attention, though. Should've been in faster. You're right about that, Daniella."

"They were fine, George." Mrs. Crieff warned.

"I thought it was a tie. I'm sure Vickie touched the wall at the same time as the other team. Didn't you, Dad? I'm gonna ask Andy what he thought." Daniella looked at Kevin and me. "You guys didn't even place, did you?"

"Nah," Kevin said then shrugged. "So they say. We thought it was a tie, right Marcie? We're checking with Andy on Monday."

"You're not funny, Kevin," Daniella said. I thought he was a riot and laughed until Daniella glared me into silence.

"Least you made it into the pool this time, Marcie," she muttered just loud enough for me to hear.

The following week Kevin and I brought canned goods to the pool everyday. All of us did. By Wednesday, our team had declared a major food war against Daniella's team. Everyone tried to win. One afternoon, Rebecca brought so many tins of tuna her swimming bag ripped.

"Let's go around the neighbourhood and collect," she suggested to Kevin. We gathered our stuff and knocked on every door for a block or two, explaining the program and asking for canned food.

When it became obvious that Lakeshore Lumber was ahead in the unofficial competition at our own pool, the morning team decided to join us.

"Our teams can canvass every house in the subdivision," Daniella told all of us after the weekend race. "How about if I write up a flyer? You guys collect."

"Why do we do the collecting?" Kevin asked. I was wondering the same thing, but no one else seemed to care.

"Well, duhhh!" Brad answered as though the reason was obvious to all thinking people. "She thought of the whole idea, Kevin. The least you guys can do is gather the food."

Daniella really had the knack for getting others to defend her.

By the time we got home, the so-called flyer had scaled down to a letter. Later that night it dwindled down again and finally turned into a note.

"What do you think?" Daniella asked, admiring her calligraphy. She sauntered across the room to my bed. I glanced at the page in her outstretched hand then grabbed the edge for a closer look. She had written the note on Crieff Construction Company letterhead.

WHAT: A food drive to support Sun Youth
WHERE: At your own front door
HOW? Leave the food in a bag outside

WHEN: Tuesday afternoon
WHY: Swimmers in our neighbourhood are collecting food to help Sun Youth feed the hungry. If we each give a little — we can do a lot.

The rest of the page was blank, except at the bottom where she had scrawled, Dan Crieff.

Daniella reached for the note. "I'll ask Andy to run this off. Brad and I can deliver the notices after practice on Monday. You guys pick up the bags the next day. Bring everything to Sun Youth. Kevin knows how to go by bus."

I had a sinking feeling in the pit of my stomach remembering my discussion with Mr. Crieff in the coffee shop. His views on feeding the homeless and roast beef for Renée.

"You can't do this, Daniella," I said.

"Why not?"

"You can't use this paper. It's letterhead for your father's company."

"For heaven sakes, Marcie! You're the one who's always whining about Renée. We need it to look official, don't we?"

"Well yeah, but . . ."

"Look, do you want to help or not?"

"Of course I want to help. Just not on this letterhead."

"Whatever!"

"Daniella, the drive's a great idea. I just don't think we should use this stationery without asking your dad. That's all."

"So, forget it then. We'll do it without you."

"No, I don't want to *forget* it. I just think your dad won't go for this." I flicked the corner of the paper then shook my head. "He won't. You should have heard him the day Kevin and I went to the warehouse with him. I couldn't believe it was your dad!"

"Mmm-hmmm." Daniella raised one eyebrow. She took hold of the page between her thumb and index finger and snapped it out of my grasp.

"I'm not saying I know your father better than you do, Daniella. Or that I don't want to help. I'll do the collecting if you ask your dad about using that paper. That's all I'm saying. It's not that I won't do anything."

When Daniella didn't answer I continued.

"Is that what you think, Daniella?"

"Oh, Marcie, you only worry about Renée when it suits you."

"That's not true, Daniella. Why would I do that?"

"I don't know. For attention, I guess. Same reason you go on all the time about your mom."

I felt the hair on my arms rise. Prickles jabbed at the back of my neck.

"What is *that* supposed to mean?"

"Oh, nothing."

"Don't say something like that and then tell me it's nothing, Daniella."

Daniella sat on the corner of her bed, her arms folded across her chest and a little smirk on her lips.

"*P-lease*, like you don't know what I'm talking about."

"No, no, I don't."

"Marcie, be honest! You're not interested in helping with the food drive. You don't care about Renée. Why should you? You don't even live in Montreal. You're more interested in getting everyone, including my brother, to feel sorry for you."

I stared at Daniella and felt my jaw tighten, my teeth clench.

"Come off it," Daniella continued. "You can't even look at the bus shelter without getting tears in your eyes. As though Renée belongs to you or something. And you're the same about your mom. It's not like she just died, Marcie. That was four years ago!"

"Daniella, she was my *mother*."

"See what I mean? You're doing it again. You're ready to cry." Daniella held her finger up, pointing to the corner of my eye as though she had somehow proved something.

"You really have no idea what it's like, do you?" I asked, slapping her finger away. "How it feels here in your house. Knowing that Vickie is across the street in *my* house. Or what it's like watching your mom. Don't you get it, Daniella? The reason I *look* upset is because I *am* upset. It still hurts. Don't you understand that?"

"Whatever you say, Marcie. It also gets you a lot of attention. That's what bugs me. And about your crusade for Renée? Well, when someone tries to help . . ."

Daniella opened her palms and shrugged.

That night, long after I heard the steady rhythm of Daniella's breathing, I pulled the covers up to my chin and stared into the blackened room. Daniella's words still stung. Did she really believe what she had said about me?

Did I?

Chapter fourteen

By the time Vickie's party rolled around, only one thing convinced me to go. The thought that Vickie had missed her real birthday. She had been thirteen for two weeks with no celebration at all.

Turning thirteen was supposed to be a big deal. Her mom should have realized that. Heck! Even *Dad* knew that! On my thirteenth birthday he had come downstairs with gold loop earrings for me.

"You're pretty grownup now, Marcie," he had said. "Mom would have wanted you to have something special today."

I wanted Vickie's thirteenth birthday to be special as well, but the last time I had been inside that house was the morning we moved. As I crossed the street with Daniella and Kevin I felt sick. What was I thinking? What was I doing?

I was going home. When the door opened I half-expected to see my own mother.

"C'mon in," Vickie greeted us.

I heard kids laughing and music blaring inside the house.

"You okay?" Kevin asked as we stepped over the stoop and the door closed behind us. Trapped. I took a deep breath. The house no longer smelled like my home. My eyes darted from corner to corner, floor to ceiling. Everything had changed. Transformed. I looked into the hallway. What had happened to Mom's dark blue wall?

I imagined it again, filling in the large opened space that stood before me now.

Vickie's mother floated forward, bursting the memory. She looked a little like Vickie, although her hair was a golden red.

"You're Marcie, aren't you?" she said with a too-sweet voice. "Vickie tells me you lived here once. Come and see the improvements we've made."

Mrs. Porter looped the tips of her ice cold fingers through my arm and I stumbled across the entrance into what was once our living room.

Beige furniture stood at odd angles, cutting off corners. At the far end, a huge window had slashed through the wall, our fireplace gone, ripped out. The whole room looked carved up and whitewashed. There were no plants. No splashes of colour. No baskets brimming with dried flowers. What had this woman done to my home?

I yanked my arm away from Mrs. Porter's icicle grip and headed for the door, pushing Kevin out of my way as I did so.

"Where ya going?" he asked reeling backward.

"Out!"

Kevin looked worried. He glanced around quickly. "Marcie, wait. I'll come with you."

I thought about the comment Daniella had made. How I wanted everyone to feel sorry for me. *Including my brother.* I'd thought about that a lot lately.

"Don't bother. Stay here!" I said and headed down the stairs. When I reached the sidewalk I spun around and shouted, "With Rebecca!"

I stormed down the street in fast-forward. Where was I going? Nowhere. I had nowhere left to go. Dad and I might have left. Mom might have died. But home was supposed to have kept going, always there, waiting across the street from the Crieffs, cradling my memories and saving them until I could step back into my life and reclaim them.

I should never have come back to Montreal. And I should never, never have gone home.

Face your fears, Dad had said. What sort of advice was that to give a kid? He had dragged me away in the first place. He had let all this happen to our house. To Mom's house.

And now what was I supposed to do? It was too early to arrive back and face Mr. and Mrs. Crieff.

I marched down the street to the park and stood at the edge of the baseball field. The park was pitch black. When I heard rustling behind me in the bushes, I spun around on my heel, opened my eyes as wide as I could and scanned the darkness. Nothing.

Just to be sure, though, I hurried out of the park, crossing the street and circling the entire block so quickly my shins hurt.

By the time I reached the glassed-in bus shelter I could hardly breathe. I went inside and sat down.

From the shelter, I heard the faint rhythm of Reggae playing at Vickie's house.

What was wrong with me? Mrs. Porter *owned* the house. Why shouldn't she change things? It wasn't her fault my mother had died. I had acted like a baby. No, worse than that. I had acted like Daniella often did. Mad and making everyone else pay for it. Why had I done that?

I had to. I had to. I answered my own thoughts. There were too many feelings colliding inside me. I dropped my head into my hands. Somehow I had betrayed Mom by going home.

Just then I sensed someone or something slip into the shelter. There was a shuffling noise and a bony hand reached out and grabbed my knee.

My stomach dropped a notch and I shrieked, recoiling to

the back of the bench. I tried to push free, but the fingers tightened on my leg.

"Wha'cha want?" the woman hissed.

I recognized the voice at once. It was Renée.

"Wha'cha want?" she repeated in a fierce whisper.

"I want Mom."

"*Arret!*" Renée held up her hand. "Shhh!" she said. Scrambling to the glass wall, she peered outside toward the street. Her eyes shifted back and forth, frightened, almost haunted, unable to rest anywhere for long.

"Cops 'ere?" she asked.

One of her arms jerked violently. She raised her hand to her neck and scratched until bleeding welts erupted on her skin. Renée reeked of alcohol or stale vomit, but she didn't appear to be drunk.

"You come for me?" Renée asked and I shook my head. Recognition flickered in her eyes then vanished. She really seemed sick. Scared. She thrust one hand toward the back of the shelter, pointing a gnarled finger at one of Daniella's Sun Youth sheets, then she narrowed her eyelids until they seemed to disappear above bloated cheeks.

"Waz' that?" she asked slowly, suspiciously. "You put that?"

I looked at the paper taped to the glass and nodded, wondering if she read English. Or any language at all. I watched her hands clench into tight fists, veins popping up on her forearm. Renée's face looked distorted.

I pushed myself further back on the wooden bench until

my shoulder blades struck the glass wall behind me. Mr. Crieff might have been right. I shouldn't be out here alone — with a lunatic.

"Renée," I spoke softly and she turned a puzzled, far away look toward me.

"It's okay, Renée. You're okay. I'm the one that put the sign there. I'm not going to hurt you. I just wanted to let you know where to get food, that's all . . . if . . . if you needed it."

I spoke quietly, afraid of insulting her. I'm not sure she understood, but the hushed tone of my voice seemed to calm her.

"Th' cops 'ere?" she whispered hoarsely again. She seemed more lucid now and I shook my head, no.

"Th' cops take me away?"

"No, Renée. No, they're not here. No one's here. Just me — Marcie Chisholm. I'm alone."

"Chiz'm?" she repeated. She said it all in one syllable, swallowing my name whole. Then she nodded. A burst of laughter escaped from Vickie's house and Renée glared through the glass wall toward the sound.

I kept talking, trying to reassure her, and trying to reassure myself at the same time. Renée flopped onto the bench beside me. She opened her mouth and laughed without sound. She really smelled terrible. Her hand fluttered up to the side of my face then away without touching me.

"I . . . know . . . you," she whispered. "You're . . . you're the girl."

Her voice sounded distant, almost hollow. She closed her eyes. Omigosh. She had recognized me. She actually remembered that horrible morning with D3. No wonder she kept asking about cops.

"Yes, that was me," I blurted out. "I didn't mean to . . . the dog didn't try to . . . it was a mistake. I should've told the police. It was my fault. My fault and I'm sorry."

Renée just sat there. She didn't move. Her eyes remained closed. In the ghostly glow cast by the streetlamp, I saw small oozing scabs raised on her lip.

"Renée? You okay?"

"Renée?"

I put two fingers on her wrist. Renée groaned. She was asleep, snoring lightly. I looked around the shelter. What a dump! Bottles, tins, old plastic bags littered the place. I considered picking everything up and tossing all of it into the trash. I changed my mind when I noticed a crumpled foil under the bench. It was the wrap that had once been around a chunk of roast beef. The food I had brought. Suddenly I felt like an intruder. This was Renée's home. These were her things.

Renée shivered beside me and a ridiculous urge to hold her crept over me. Instead, I took off my denim jacket and spread it gently across her shoulders. Quietly, I tiptoed out of the shelter where Renée lived.

Outside, I gasped for air and made my way toward the Crieffs' house. I hadn't gotten far when I noticed a figure on the curb across the street. He spotted me and stood, walking toward me.

"I don't wanna be with Rebecca," he said.

Chapter fifteen

There were two races left and my team lost both. After the final race, Andy thanked everyone, especially the team sponsors. He then called upon Mr. Crieff to present awards. A medallion suspended on a tricolour ribbon was given to each swimmer on the winning team.

"Daniella Crieff, Brad Dupuis, Ajay Kapoor, Vickie Porter, Chet Baklar," Andy shouted into a megaphone. The five swimmers walked forward while the rest of us clapped.

Finally, someone spoke about our efforts collecting food for the homeless and the hungry. And that was it. Swimming was over for the summer. I had not wanted to join at first, but now wished our practices would never end.

When we got home Daniella hung the enormous medallion she had won on the front of the fridge. A reminder to the rest of us whenever we ate.

The following weekend Sammy called and invited Kevin and me to a team party. "A barbecue at my house. Just a little get-together to end the season," he explained.

It poured rain the day of the barbecue.

"Let's go anyway," Kevin suggested.

We took the city bus along Jean Talon until we saw the metro station at Décarie. Sammy's house was a short walk from the metro.

Inside the front door Kevin and I kicked off our shoes, heaping them on top of a pile that was already there. We found the others by following the sound of music and Rebecca's laugh. The party was in a small wood-panelled room at the end of the hall, down a short flight of stairs.

Rebecca sat on a gold and green couch near the entrance. Her legs stretched over most of the cushions and across Tony's knees. Tony pummelled Rebecca's feet with a pillow.

"Move those smelly toes over!"

The whole team had showed up. Sammy and Marc stood at the patio door. Seeing us, Sammy dashed out the sliding glass door into the drizzle and returned with two semi-damp hamburgers. Before long, everyone was munching on burgers and talking at once, shouting now and again to be heard.

Sammy's wife, Rachel, squeezed through the doorway and

into the room. She wore knee-length walking shorts and a navy shirt and she carried a tray loaded with Cokes.

"Hello! You must be Kevin and Marcie. It's great to meet you, but I wish all of you could have come on another day," she said. "The yard is quite pleasant when it's nice out."

"Nah, this is fine, Rachel," Sammy joked. "Rain doesn't hurt this team. They're all washed up anyway."

Tony picked up his pounding pillow and whipped it across the room at Sammy. "Oh yeah? We'd have done a lot better if we had a real coach! Anyhow, we could have been faster if we had wanted, right guys? It was good planning on our part. Gave us easier teams to compete against in those horrendous races."

Tony tapped the side of his temple with his index finger and narrowed his eyes. "Strategy!"

We hooted with laughter and all agreed.

"Team strategy," Marc repeated and Rebecca pointed a half-eaten burger at me.

"We should've taken Marcie's lead. If the whole team had fainted when we saw what we were up against, we might have been totally disqualified and had the whole summer to goof off."

I made a small clucking sound with my tongue. "I did my best to warn you. The message was just too subtle for you guys, I guess."

"I guess," Sammy said. "When do you go back to Toronto? Must be pretty soon."

"Really soon. I can't believe how fast the summer zoomed by."

Sammy nodded. "No kidding. Shows we had fun. We'll miss you when you leave Montreal, Marcie."

"Yeah, some of us more than others. Right, Kevin?" Tony teased.

Kevin was across the room tossing darts into a board, his back toward us. He turned to face Tony and grinned. I'd been trying not to think about leaving. Funny how things change. I glanced around at the others.

Everyone looked different without swimsuits and those black and orange shirts, all wearing jeans, and all stretched out around Sammy's recreation room instead of the pool. But they still looked like a team — my team.

Just before the party ended, Rachel walked into the room again.

"He's here, dear," she said quietly to Sammy.

Sammy nodded and climbed the three stairs leading out of the basement before he disappeared into the kitchen. When he returned, an older man followed him down the steps.

"Watch your head, Carl," Sammy warned and the man ducked as he came into the room. He wore faded jeans, black glasses and a Lakeshore Lumber t-shirt. His arms were outstretched, holding a cardboard box. A striped dishtowel was draped over several lumps in the box, hiding whatever lay underneath.

"Kids, I'd like to introduce Carl Vachon," Sammy announced, reaching out a hand and clapping the other man on the shoulder blade. "Some of you may have seen Carl before. He's been to every meet. Carl is the one who supplied your shirts and sponsored our team."

"Alright!" Rebecca called and we all cheered.

"Sorry I wasn't here earlier. I could have made it to the barbecue, but I was sure it would be postponed," Carl explained, pretending to shake rain off his balding head.

"Hope you kids had a good summer," he said. "I know I did. I went to every race, as Sammy says, and I enjoyed every one. You were a great team. You couldn't seem to win. Not once. But you never stopped trying."

Carl Vachon looked from one Lakeshore Lumber swimmer to the next. When he got to me, I thought he smiled a bit before he continued.

"You made me proud. Proud of your spirit. Proud of your effort and proud to have my company's name on your shirts."

I felt a lump in my throat and looked over at Rebecca. She was turned away, gently rubbing her eye with two fingers.

Carl placed the package he carried on Sammy's desk. He took off the dishtowel and smiled. Five small golden trophies stood inside the box.

"You're champions in my eyes," Carl said. "Every one of you."

I have placed in violin contests before and I've even won a couple of plaques for doing well at school, but in my whole life I have never won a trophy for sports.

I felt the small firm figure in my hand. A golden swimmer, arms stretched high in the air, ready to dive off a black stand. We had lost every race and the last thing I expected was an award. Yet here it was. My very own trophy. Losing had never felt like this before.

When we got home, Kevin and I positioned our swimmers, one on each side of the fridge.

"What are those for?" Daniella asked.

Kevin beamed. "Trophies from our sponsor. Our whole team got one."

"Trophies?" Daniella slowly repeated. "For all of you? What on earth for? You guys didn't win a race. Marcie can hardly swim!"

I watched the light bounce off the golden head of my trophy and smiled. I could hardly wait to show Dad.

Shortly after our little swimmers arrived, Daniella removed her tricolour ribbon draped across the front of the fridge.

We never saw the medallion again.

Chapter sixteen

A couple of days before I was scheduled to leave, I carried a bag full of food down the street to the bus shelter. I really hadn't brought much since the day Mr. Crieff told me not to interfere, but I would be going back to Toronto soon. Besides, I wasn't sure that Sun Youth knew about Renée, and I couldn't leave Montreal without giving her something.

I didn't want to embarrass her though. When I got to the bus stop, I walked by, staring ahead. A couple of steps past the shelter, I glanced over my shoulder to check for Renée. She was there all right. Lying on the cement — face down.

Dropping the food, I ran into the shelter and knelt by Renée.

"Renée? Renée!"

There was no response.

"Are you okay?" I shouted. Hearing a mumbling sound, I tried to flip Renée onto her side. I could hardly budge her. When I finally managed to turn her face and upper body, I noticed my denim jacket rolled into a pillow under her head. It was covered in blood.

"Help! Help me!" I screamed at the top of my voice and jumped to my feet. Renée moved her hand.

"Wait," she whispered.

I could scarcely hear and scrambled down beside her, leaning forward, lowering my head to her face. "Renée, you're bleeding. You've fallen or something and cut your head. I've got to get help."

"Wait," she moaned. "Give . . . t' . . . you."

Renée seemed to be talking underneath her voice, gasping for air between each word. She stretched a shaking hand forward.

"Take . . . take la," she mumbled, pressing something cold into my palm.

"Help me!" I screamed again, but there was no one in sight and no one came.

"Renée, I'm going for help. Hold on."

I sprang up again and this time charged down the street toward home. I took the steps two at a time, then pushed opened the heavy oak door. My breath escaped in bursts of pain and my pulse hammered a dry throat.

"Call 911!" I screamed, darting through the kitchen,

along a narrow hall and up the back stairs. "Call the police!"

I burst through the door of my old bedroom, not even realizing where I had run until Vickie looked up from her bed.

"What's wrong, Marcie?" she asked, springing onto her feet and knocking her phone off the bedside table. "What are you doing over here? What's happened?"

"Renée," I gasped. "Renée . . . hurt. You . . . think she'll die? Vickie, will she die?" I dug my fingers into Vickie's arm and pulled her toward the bedroom door.

"Marcie, calm down! Calm down! We'll call for help from here. Where is she?"

"Bus shelter," I shouted, trying to point toward the street. My hand shook and my teeth chattered. Vickie pushed me down onto the side of the bed. She grabbed her phone from the floor and dialled 911. When she had given the location, she threw a quilt around my shoulders. I stretched out my fingers and grabbed it. There was a soft clinking sound on the floor beside the bed.

"We'd better go back and wait for the ambulance," Vickie said.

"Omigosh. That's right. They'll send an ambulance."

"Marcie, it's okay. I'll go with you." Vickie shoved her toes into sandals. "Where the heck is Daniella?" she asked.

"Out. Saint Leonard. It's her Grandpa's f-funeral. No, no, I m-mean b-birthday."

It was not cold, but my teeth knocked against each other as though I was out in a snowstorm. My body twitched in sharp, jerking movements. The way it had when my mother died. I could scarcely squeeze my words out, and clenched my molars together, trying to stop that awful shivering before I continued.

"Th . . . they all w-went. I st-stayed home. Wanted to . . . to . . . sort my stuff."

Vickie ran into the hall.

"You coming?"

I clutched the edge of the quilt tightly.

"I can't," I whispered, but Vickie was already at the top of the stairs.

"Marcie, come on!"

"Vickie, I . . . I."

I tried to move, but my shoes felt stapled to the hardwood floor. I could not force my feet to follow Vickie into the hall.

"I can't," I whispered hoarsely as my mind rewound and replayed the ambulance ride I'd taken four years before.

"Marcie, please!" Vickie pleaded, reappearing at the bedroom door. "You have to come. Renée doesn't even know me."

Suddenly, the image in my mind switched to Renée face down in the bus shelter. Then, for no reason at all, I pictured a golden swimmer. *You couldn't seem to win, but you never stopped trying.*

When we got back to the shelter, Renée had rolled from my jacket and was lying on cement. I crouched down beside her, pulling the jacket toward her head.

"Hold on, Renée. It's me. It's Marcie."

"Don't try to move her, Marcie. She's in bad shape," Vickie said. She paced back and forth from Renée to the glass wall of the shelter, scanning the street in both directions. "Where are they? What's taking them so long?"

My hand under Renée's head cramped. Pins-and-needles crept from the tips of my fingers up my arm. Renée's lids were half-open and all I could see were the whites of her eyes. I focused on Renée while in my mind another scene played out.

Vickie and I both jumped when we heard the faint whine of a siren.

"They're here!" Vickie shouted and bolted out of the shelter and onto the street, waving both arms above her head.

I kept my eyes on Renée.

"They're here, Renée," I whispered softly next to her ear.

I waited until I heard the closeness of voices, and the bump of a hospital cot as it rolled quickly into the shelter. Gently, I moved my hand from beneath Renée's head and stepped onto the grass outside.

Vickie and I watched the attendants lower the bed for Renée.

"She has a head wound here, André," one said.

"Yeah, I see that. From the looks of her, this woman didn't lead a very healthy life. Ready? Let's get her onto the bed, Josée."

André snapped an oxygen mask over Renée's face while Josée covered her with a gray hospital blanket. They pulled two thick canvas straps from under the frame of the bed, cinching them together, one across Renée's legs and the other over her chest. All the while, the static sound of a dispatch radio snapped on and off in the vehicle behind me.

"How long's she been like this?" one of the medics called over his shoulder, his fingers searching for the pulse in Renée's wrist.

"Maybe fifteen, twenty minutes," Vickie answered.

"What's her name?"

"Renée," Vickie said then looked at me and frowned. "We don't know her last name."

"The police do," I said. "One of them talked to Renée right here about eight weeks ago."

The second attendant nodded. She took a few steps out of the shelter and reached for the ambulance radio. "You the one that made the call?" she asked.

I shook my head and pointed to Vickie then moved away from the sight and sound of the radio. Ambulance lights raced after me, streaking across the glass wall of the shelter before bouncing back over the sidewalk and circling my legs.

My knees were rubber and my body had started to twitch again. I sat down at the curb and waited until the attendants had wheeled Renée out to the ambulance and closed the rear door.

After answering a couple of questions, Vickie joined me

on the curb, her arm warm on my back. Together we watched the red tail lights disappear around the corner at the far end of the block. Neither of us moved until the scream of the siren had melted into silence.

Chapter seventeen

We walked back to Vickie's house without speaking and I collapsed onto a chair in her kitchen. My body shook and the tips of my fingers felt numb.

"Here, have this," Vickie said.

I wrapped both hands around the warm mug and breathed in the steam spiralling upward from my tea.

"W-where's your mom?" I asked. "S-she here?"

"Nah. She's at work," Vickie answered.

"This thing with Renée? Today in the shelter? That's how m-my mom died, Vickie. An ambulance came for her and I never saw her again." My voice sounded far off and tinny. Vickie nodded, her eyes misted.

"That day felt like the end of the earth. I was with someone. A nurse maybe . . . or no . . . I guess it was a neighbour. Someone who used to live down the street, I think. She'd been at the hospital, recognized me, stayed with me until Dad arrived. Later, when Dad told me what happened to Mom, it was as though he had said, the world will end today, Marcie."

Vickie set down her tea and wrapped an arm around my shoulder.

"I was there when the accident happened, Vickie. With Mom. She was hit on Côte-des-Neiges. A car came around the corner on a red light and didn't stop. Mom and I were crossing and she pushed me out of the way. Afterward, months later, I started thinking maybe I could have done something. You know. Saved her."

"No, no, Marcie, what, what could you have done?"

Vickie had a hard time speaking and when I looked up, I saw the tears.

"Marcie, why don't you look around the house, alone? Would you like to do that?"

"Could I do that? Would it be all right?"

Vickie nodded. "I'll stay in my room. Take as long as you want."

Spreading my fingers, I ran my hand along walls, under railings. I counted steps from one room to the next. It took a while. My mind was a video camera, scanning each room, zooming in here and there. Focusing. Remembering.

I imagined Mom and Dad, too, as I framed the mental pictures I would carry away with me. The counter in the kitchen where Mom had rolled cookie dough. The adjoining dining room. A narrow stained glass window above the front door. Stairs in the front hall that Kevin and I used to toboggan down until Dad stopped us.

Sitting again on the top step, I bumped all the way down to the basement. At the bottom was a cold room for storing fruit and vegetables. It had its own smell. Like mud in the spring when it rains. The shelves were empty now. No pickles. No jelly. Nothing.

I squatted beside the built-in bins and scooped up two or three onions with green shoots growing out the tops. There were no potatoes at all.

Leaning against the door, I thought of something and spun around, checking, sliding my palm along the smooth wood that framed the door. I pressed my index finger into a small notch then moved my hand a bit lower. There was another. A third, lower still. My birthday notches!

The notches Dad had etched every year to measure my height. They were still scratched into the wood. *Yes!* This had been my home and it still held a record of me.

With the heels of my feet pressing the door frame, I leaned backward, my hand straight from the top of my head to the wooden frame behind. My fingers touched high above the last mark. By now, I could almost hear my mother's voice. *Oh my gosh, Marcie, you're a giant! Look how much you've grown!* It was the first time I'd remembered that birthday routine in nearly four years.

Outside Mom's room, I stood for a long time before slowly, slowly, turning the handle. Gauze curtains hung at the window. There was a large bed positioned diagonally in the middle of the room. White bedspread. Thick rugs.

Where was the clutter?

A pale shawl draped a wooden chest at the foot of the bed, but that was all. This was not my mother's room. There were no clothes tossed on a rocker. No bright blue cushions thrown on the bed. Tiny glass figures no longer danced over a dresser. And the pink pie-plate mold of my handprint no longer hung on the wall.

I studied the room once more before finally closing the door. This was not my mother's room and this was no longer my home. My home was in Toronto with Dad, or maybe even in Montreal with the Crieffs, but it was no longer here. A friend lived in this house now.

A laugh bubbled inside my stomach when I walked out of Vickie's house. I had the free feeling I sometimes get on the last day of school. I'd just reached the Crieffs' house when Vickie crossed the street. She held out a dull metal object.

"This yours?"

I frowned and picked the small oval from her palm.

"I found it beside my bed. Did you drop it?"

"Renée just gave me that. I forgot all about it."

I rubbed the grimy metal with my thumb until a few flecks of red stone glistened. I fumbled with the clasp, but even before it released, I knew I had seen that locket before.

"Marcie? Are you sure it's the same one?" Vickie asked in the Crieffs' kitchen a while later. A jar of silver cleaner and the flat box filled with Mom's treasures lay on the counter between us.

"It has to be, Vickie."

There wasn't a picture of Dad inside to prove it or anything, but to me, there was no doubt. Several of the stones were missing, but it looked just like the locket Mom wore in the photo that Mrs. Crieff had given me.

"See for yourself," I said, shoving the little box of Mom's treasures toward Vickie. "Take out the picture again. Doesn't that look like the same locket?"

Vickie squinted at the photo of my mother and nodded. "It does."

Picking up the locket, she examined it closely, comparing it to the one in the picture. "Maybe this one isn't your mom's, though. There must be hundreds of them all alike."

"It is. It has to be."

"Marcie, think about it. How would a bag lady in a bus shelter have your mother's locket?"

"I dunno."

I slumped my shoulders. We'd been over it a hundred times already. How had the locket ended up among Renée's treasures? I kept hoping she had found the locket. Picked it up from the mountain of trash that had lined the curb outside our house before we moved. But I had my doubts.

I know you. You're the girl, Renée had said the night of Vickie's party. There was no question that she had known Mom, or at least seen her, maybe known where she lived. Then today she had given the locket to me.

"I think she stole it."

Vickie shrugged. "Maybe she did. Who knows."

I slid my thumb back and forth across the locket. What had happened to the heavy silver chain? Renée had probably hawked it.

"Marcie, you're never going to find out for sure. What's most important to you? That Renée took it? Or that she gave it back?"

I thought about those questions after Vickie left, but I already knew the answer. Because of Renée, I felt connected to Mom. The locket hung around my neck on a shoelace. I was wearing the same jewellery my mother had worn. Or, at least, I thought I was.

D3 nudged my thigh with his forepaws and I let him out into the yard. Then I phoned Vickie.

"Hi, Vic. It's me, again. Listen, would you watch for the Crieffs' car?"

"Okay."

"I can't write all this in a note. When they get home, do you think you could explain it to Mrs. Crieff?"

"If you want me to. Yeah. I could."

"Tell her what happened, okay? Tell all of it. About the locket. The ambulance. All of it. I can't explain why, Vickie, but I really need to go down to the hospital."

"Oh, Marcie."

"I know. It's just something I have to do. Tell her, okay."

"Yes, I will. But are you all right to go alone?"

"I am. I'm fine. I'll talk to you later."

"Good luck."

"Thank you, Vickie. For everything."

In the afternoons, the wait for a bus downtown doesn't take long. I stood on the curb outside Renée's little shelter and faced the street. Before long, a city bus lumbered toward me.

Not long after the door swooshed shut behind me, we headed down Côte-des-Neiges toward the hospital. I was too late for Mom, but maybe not for Renée, and I didn't want her to be alone. Not now.

Chapter eighteen

Finding Renée wasn't that easy.

I couldn't speak French, didn't know her last name, and had a hard time explaining why I was looking. Besides, the emergency ward was crowded and almost everyone I spoke to sent me into the waiting room to wait.

Every time the door into the medical area swung open, I rocked forward in my chair, trying to spot Renée before the door closed. Narrow beds lined both sides of the inner hall, but I was too far away to recognize patients. I must have sat there for over an hour, and then, finally, I heard a noise that I recognized.

It was the sound of a siren.

I am almost positive the receptionist rolled her eyes when she saw me jump up again. I approached her desk anyway.

"Is Josée here? The paramedic who works on the ambulance?"

"Josée? Josée LeDuc? *Non, pas maintenant.* Just wait. She'll be back."

Josée remembered Renée. And she remembered me too. Things changed after that. This time, after speaking to Josée, the receptionist picked up the phone. A moment later she said to me, "Renée Peltier is being admitted. It'll be a while before you can go up to her ward. Wait in the waiting room upstairs, if you like."

When I saw Renée, I scarcely recognized her. Clear fluid dripped from a plastic bag at the side of her bed, along a tube, and into her arm. She wore a hospital gown, and a cap hid her matted hair. Her face was scrubbed and younger looking, nearly a third of it hidden behind an oxygen mask.

"She can't talk. Are you family?" a voice behind me asked.

"Sort of."

The nurse pushed back the curtain surrounding the bed. She looked at me and raised her eyebrows. Then she pulled a black band out of her pocket and wrapped it around Renée's arm, pressing a silver disk under the cuff. I waited while she took Renée's blood pressure.

"Well, no, I'm not family," I admitted when I heard the snap of Velcro release Renée's arm. "But I want to stay with her."

The nurse wrote something on a small notepad before looking at me again.

"Okay. Just don't try to wake her."

I nodded and dragged a chair close to the bed. I fought a gagging sensation at the base of my throat. There was a strong smell of cleanser or medicine in the cramped cubicle. Every twenty minutes or so, the nurse popped her head around the curtain. After the fourth time, she changed the bag dripping into Renée's arm.

"You still here?" she asked.

"Is she going to die?" I answered.

"We're trying to make her comfortable," the nurse said, adjusting Renée's pillows. I didn't like the sound of that. Every time she came in, I asked the same question.

"She's not doing well. How do you know her?"

I told the story. How I'd met Renée. Seeing her at the mall. How I'd tried to gather food to give to Sun Youth to feed the hungry. How I thought Renée had known Mom. The next time I asked if Renée would die, the nurse told me she would.

Around six o'clock, her head poked around the curtain again.

"There's a coffee shop on the main floor."

My stomach tightened, growling at the memory of food.

"I'm not too hungry," I lied. I had left the Crieffs' house with bus tickets, but without any money. A short time later, the nurse reappeared with a can of pop and a small tub of vanilla ice cream.

"This oughta' keep you going for awhile. I'm off now, but Marie's on duty. Call her if you need help." She pointed to a black buzzer attached to the side rail of Renée's bed.

I liked Marie. She answered my questions and kept checking Renée. "Marcie, Renée doesn't have a lot of time left. Why don't you go into the lounge now."

Instead, I leaned forward, watching Renée. I wondered how old she was. Where she was from. How she had known Mom. I knew very little about the woman, but I did know what I wanted to do. What I wished I had been able to do when Mom died. I stretched out my fingers and held Renée's hand.

"I'm here Renée. You're not alone," I whispered close to her ear then jumped back startled when a phone on the night stand beside me rang. It was Mrs. Crieff.

"I'm on my way down, Marcie. I'll bring you home."

"I need to stay here." There was a long pause.

"I don't think so, Marcie."

"Please, Mrs. Crieff. I have to."

Another long wait before Mrs. Crieff finally spoke.

"Marcie, I can't leave you there alone. If you're determined to stay then I'll come down and sit with you."

"Mrs. Crieff?" I said just before I hung up, "Do you think you could bring my violin with you?"

"I'm not sure that's a good idea, Marcie," Mrs. Crieff said gently. But when she walked into the room half an hour later she had the violin tucked under her arm. She put the case down beside my chair and gave my shoulder a gentle squeeze before going to Renée's bed.

"My gosh! I know this woman," Mrs. Crieff half-turned toward me. "She used to work around our neighbourhood. You know, she did cleaning jobs. Washed windows, that sort of thing. She was a bit of a lost soul even then."

"You knew Renée?"

"Renée, yes, that was her first name. She's listed here as Peltier, but her name used to be Gauche, Gaucherie, something like that. She did a lot of work down the block at Mrs. Joyce's place. She did a few things for us too, but not much. Renée worked for your Mom once in awhile, though. Do you remember her?"

A memory tugged from the underside of my thoughts. "Wait a minute. Someone stayed with us for a couple of months the year Mom broke her leg."

"No, that was someone else. Renée was long before that. You'd have been too young to remember, I guess. She didn't live with you, just came in every now and again and worked for the day. She lived somewhere around Décarie. Her husband worked over at the track."

"She was married?"

"For awhile. Something happened. I forget the whole story. Someone in George's company used to know them. They were quite a pair! Apparently the husband was drinking one night and burned their place down. They had no insurance.

"Renée started out okay. She was a hard worker at first,

but she turned out to be totally unreliable. You know the type. She'd tell you she'd be there, then not show up. Or she'd show up reeking of alcohol, that sort of thing. Eventually things started disappearing and it always seemed to be after Renée had been around."

Mrs. Crieff made a clucking sound with her tongue as she watched Renée.

"I heard she'd moved off somewhere. Never thought much about her again, until today. Your mom tried to help Renée, give her jobs, talk to her about being on time. We all did. We didn't get much thanks for it, though. Renée never appreciated anything anyone tried to do for her. I don't believe she ever did a kindness in return."

My hand went to the silver locket around my neck, the tips of my fingers searching the stones.

"She did once," I said.

Chapter nineteen

I took out my violin and played.

My favourite piece. *Spring.* The first movement in Vivaldi's *Four Seasons.* One I had played in competition dozens of times. I had practised a lot and it didn't sound bad, the strings of my violin quivering as the bow slid back and forth like a skater on a sheet of ice.

I played for Renée and for Mom. For a lost home. For myself. And, finally, for the music itself which seemed to lift me higher and higher until I no longer felt it in my body, but floating, spiralling somewhere outside the hospital.

I played in spurts. Parts I remembered. Bits I made up. The notes blended one into the next like a quilt. I closed my eyes and pictured the music. The cracking of ice on a pond. Morning. The smell of an opening bud. The sun on my face. Birds. The tip of an icicle dripping, slowly at first. A stream. Then the rush of a waterfall. And back to a pond. To my mom. And my dad. To me.

I felt the room swell with people. Someone behind me started to hum. Somebody cried. When I opened my eyes, someone nodded. And somebody smiled.

Renée died that night at 10:23.

She never opened her eyes. Never saw us. Her breathing slowed and slowed until it finally stopped. It was peaceful. Almost as though Renée had fallen asleep.

Mrs. Crieff said she was sure Renée knew we were there. I don't know if she did, or even if she heard me play. I hope that she did.

It was late when we left the hospital, but Mrs. Crieff drove farther downtown.

"Let's get a bite to eat before we go home, Marcie. What do you say?"

I nodded and we circled around until we found a place to park. Inside the delicatessen I told Mrs. Crieff the story of Mom's locket.

"I guess Renée stole it. What I still don't understand, though, was how on earth she connected me to Mom."

Mrs. Crieff smiled.

"Marcie, do you have any idea, dear, how much you look like your mom?" I thought of the photo. Mom would have looked just like me when Renée had known her.

"I'm sorry about Renée, Marcie. And I am so sorry for what you went through with your mom. She meant a lot to me. You and your father both. I've known your family, Marcie, since you were a tiny baby, but I don't think I realized, until this evening, what a strong young woman you have become."

Mrs. Crieff's words wrapped around me like a warm blanket. I looked up at her. Before me was the answer to a riddle that had puzzled me all summer — *What had I ever liked about Daniella Crieff?* It was her family. All of them.

"Do you know why Dad sent me here, Mrs. Crieff?" I asked suddenly. "I've hardly heard from him all summer."

Mrs. Crieff put down her napkin and nodded.

"How much do you remember about your mom's accident, Marcie?" she asked.

I thought about a green car careening around the corner at Côte-des-Neiges against the light. I heard again the squeal of brakes. The screaming. The wail of the ambulance. The ride to the hospital. I saw it in my mind. Heard again the questions the police asked. Remembered that feeling of watching a real-life movie racing, too fast, on the screen ahead. For the first time, though, I let the whole scene replay. All of it. I relived it all.

Not once did I get that fuzzy-headed feeling. Maybe, instead of *not thinking* about it, *thinking* about it, *talking* about it was exactly what I should have been doing all along.

"I remember most of it, now," I answered truthfully. "Why?"

"When your mother died, Marcie, neither you nor your father could think about it for a very long time. Your father couldn't bring himself to talk about it at all. That's understandable. I'm not criticizing. It's just that, well, sometimes, burying it all, only helps for a little while.

"Your dad began to realize that not too long ago. Last year on his way home from an assignment in Vermont, he stopped in Montreal. He went through a lot of the emotions you've gone through this summer. Not Renée, or anything like that, but, you know, back to the old neighbourhood, that sort of thing.

"Before he left, your dad came to see me, to suggest bringing you to our house for a visit. He thought you might need time here, Marcie, and of course we wanted to see you, too. When your father had to go to the States for work, I suggested that you still come alone. Your father agreed. That's why you're here."

It's funny how things work out. Spending a summer in Montreal was the last thing I had wanted, yet I had learned so much about Mom in the past few weeks. And I had learned a few things about myself, as well. It was after midnight by the time we drove up the driveway. My head seemed to weigh a lot and I couldn't stop yawning, but there was someone I needed to call.

"Marcie, are you okay? What's wrong?"

"I'm sorry I woke you, Dad."

"You didn't. I'm busy typing up an assignment. Everything alright?"

"Yes. Dad? Can we talk a few minutes?"

"Now? What about?"

"Mom."

There was a muffled sound on the line. Then silence. As though no one was there. "Dad?" I said softly. No one answered. I was about to hang up when he finally spoke.

"Just a minute, Marcie. I'll turn off the computer."

I was really tired by the time we hung up. Groping around the bedroom, I found a nightie to wear. I had just placed my locket on the nightstand beside me and crawled into bed when Daniella sat up.

"She die?"

"Yeah. Tonight."

"Were you grossed out?"

I remembered how peaceful it had been at the hospital.

"No, it wasn't like that, Daniella."

Daniella turned on the lamp beside her bed. I repeated what I had just told my father. "I was scared but glad I was there. It was okay." I didn't tell Daniella about my chattering teeth at Vickie's house, or how frightened I had been at the shelter.

"I'd have died. I mean it. When Vickie told me what happened, all I could think of was how thankful I was that *we* weren't here when you found her!"

I laughed.

"You're so honest, Daniella."

Daniella climbed out of bed and staggered across the room. She stretched out her hand and lifted my locket.

"Pretty. Wonder why she didn't sell it? I mean, she obviously needed money."

"Yeah, I know. I thought of that, too. Maybe she forgot that she had it. Or just wanted something of her own. Who knows?"

Who *did* know — only Renée. Maybe it was because she liked Mom. Or remembered that Mom had been kind. Maybe Mom was as close to family as Renée had ever gotten.

"Creepy," Daniella said and I heard the locket drop back into place. "How can you wear it? Doesn't it make you angry? I mean that it was your mother's locket and Renée stole it?"

"No, it doesn't make me angry," I answered truthfully. I had forgiven Renée for whatever she'd done. Sounds strange, but I felt as though, sometime tonight at the hospital, I had also forgiven myself. Vickie was right. There was probably nothing I could have done to save Mom. I had done my best.

"For all we know, Daniella, my mother might have given her the locket. Let's go to sleep now. I'm really tired. We'll talk tomorrow. Okay?"

"I'd have been furious. I mean, it belonged to your mother and you might never have gotten it back. Marcie? You asleep?"

"Yep," I said, but Daniella kept talking. Finally, I rolled

over onto my side and popped a pillow over my ear.

"It's not like Renée was family, Marcie? Marcie? Marcie, you awake . . . ?"

Chapter twenty

The day before I left, I ran around the entire house looking for my stuff. Mrs. Crieff had washed most of my clothes and they were folded on my bed. Still, there were a couple of things I was missing.

Downstairs, I heard Daniella mention to Kevin about Renée. They flipped back and forth from English to French in that combined language they both spoke. The amazing thing was that I now understood it.

"Is Marcie awake?" Kevin asked.

"She's awake!" I called down the stairs. "Stop talking about me."

Kevin laughed.

"I thought you couldn't speak French, Marcie," Daniella said.

"Oh-oh! Now we really can't talk about her," Kevin added. "Come and tell me what happened last night, Marcie. I want details!"

A while later a car door slammed and I opened the front door for Mr. Crieff. He smiled but waited by the car as Mrs. Porter crossed the street.

"Hello, George."

"How are you, Babs?"

"Did you hear the news?"

"What news? Heard plenty of news today and don't like any of it." Mr. Crieff pulled a paper from the inside pocket of his jacket.

"Apparently there was a lot of nonsense last night about some street woman, then, this morning, I ran into Brad's mother. She showed me this!"

Mr. Crieff snapped the paper in his hand. I knew what it was.

"Daniella," I whispered. "You'd better come out here."

"What in tarnation do you make of this?" Mr. Crieff grumbled, waving the food flyer. "My company name is plastered all over it!"

"Uhh, I think I might know what that is, Dad." Kevin shifted from one foot to the other in the doorway.

I continued, "Mr. Crieff . . . I . . . we, we were donating to that bucket at th' . . ."

"I *told* you to lay off that stuff, Marcie." Mr. Crieff hit the back of his knuckles against the corner of the page. "This is written on company letterhead!"

Daniella strolled onto the driveway and stood between her father and Mrs. Porter.

"Hi, Babs," she said then turned to her father. "This was my idea, Dad."

Daniella's fingers stretched toward the letterhead. "What's wrong with it?"

"Your idea? Your idea?" Mr. Crieff repeated. "What were you thinking? You must know you can't use my name."

"I used my own name," Daniella replied. "I signed Dan Crieff." She pointed to the signature on the bottom line. "I shouldn't have used letterhead. I should have asked you, I guess."

"You *guess?*"

I'm sure it would have gotten a lot worse if Babs Porter hadn't interrupted.

"Well, never mind about that, now, George. You'll like this news. There was a little piece on TV about that street person you were talking about. They got some information from the hospital, apparently. I didn't think much of it until this morning when I got a call from the paper. Vickie phoned the police you know."

"No, no, I didn't, Babs. I don't know a lot of things that go on around here, it seems. Come inside. Have a seat."

Mr. Crieff walked into the living room behind Mrs. Porter

and we followed. Daniella pulled a wood-backed chair close to Mrs. Porter, but Kevin and I stood by the door.

"Hello, Kevin," Mrs. Porter said through a straight-line smile drawn across her mouth with lipstick. She looked at me and nodded. "Well, Marsha. You certainly look a lot better than the last time we met."

"Marcie," I corrected.

"So, Vickie called the police?" Mr. Crieff said, prompting Mrs. Porter to continue.

"Yes, yes she did. As I was saying, the paper called early this morning. They're planning an in-depth story on the need for improved shelters I think, or was it some other form of assistance for the homeless? Oh well, it's always something, isn't it? Anyway, they want to include a bit about responsible teens."

Mr. Crieff's eyebrows shot up and he snorted.

"George, I'm in marketing. You're in construction. Bit of free exposure never hurt business."

"No, s'pose not," Mr. Crieff agreed. "The kids really did try to help, Babs. My daughter, here, made flyers."

"We were trying to get food. You know, that program they run at the pool every year, Babs? To support Sun Youth?" Daniella waved a hand in our direction without turning her head. "They worked on it, too."

Mrs. Porter clapped those small, ice-cold hands of hers together.

"Good for you, Daniella. That shows initiative. Anyway,

George, the paper got a copy of the flyer. A reporter plans to contact you about your role in all this. Asked me what I knew about the food drive. Of course, what could I tell them? I really don't keep up on everything that goes on around town."

"No. Well, I don't know much more, Babs. But, I'm glad to add my two cents. But, Daniella, don't let me ever find out that you've taken my letterhead again. Or else!"

We never did find out what would happen. Probably nothing. Daniella Crieff is the only kid I know who can be grounded and ungrounded before she's even left a room.

Later that day Vickie stopped over.

"See the news, Marcie?"

"I heard about it. Your mom stopped by."

"They think I did it all. I haven't owned up yet, but I will. I should have told them you were the one who did everything right away. It's just Mom was so proud, you know, saying . . ."

"Don't tell her anything more," I interrupted. I thought about Vickie racing out to help Renée, making tea for me and letting me wander through her house alone.

"Don't say anything about me, Vickie. Things are working out and if the story actually gets in the paper, a lot of people will read it. That's bound to bring donations of food, or some other help for homeless people. Anyway, you *were* the one who called the ambulance."

I woke the next morning to the sound of *Bang, Bang,*

Bang and jumped up, excited that I would soon be back in Toronto. Would soon see Dad.

It'd been eight weeks and I was almost glad to be going home. *Almost,* but not *quite!* There were a few reasons why I didn't want to leave . . . and one of them was out on the driveway throwing a basketball against the garage.

Daniella tossed her nest of blankets onto the floor and opened the window.

"Cut it out, Kevin!" she yelled.

I stuffed clothes into my backpack. Wrapped my golden swimmer inside the team shirt and positioned it carefully on top of my clothes. With everything squeezed inside, I pulled and knotted the drawstrings. It had been a good summer. Make that a great summer.

"I'll miss you," Daniella said, yawning. She watched me slip the shoelace over my head and tuck Mom's locket inside my shirt.

"Yeah, right," I answered.

Daniella laughed.

"No, really. You're okay."

I put the knapsack beside my violin by the door and looked at Daniella.

"Yeah, you can have your room back now, Daniella. And you can also have back the pleasure of D3."

"Oh, no. I'd forgotten about D3."

This time we both laughed.

I went outside and stood by the edge of the grass. Kevin was bouncing the basketball, slamming it through the hoop every now and again. Good grief. I had already started to miss him and I hadn't even left yet.

"Will you call me, Kevin?"

"Nah!" He said then grinned. "You call me?"

"Nah!" I answered.

Kevin shot the ball at me then came over to retrieve it, tossing it onto the lawn. He rested his forearms on my shoulders, his hands laced behind my neck.

"I'm really going to miss you," I whispered and he nodded.

"I'll email you. I don't know how often, though, but I'll call sometimes. Okay?"

"Okay."

I pulled Kevin toward me into a quick hug. His heart was thumping, I think, but it might have been mine. "Thanks for being such a good friend, Kevin," I whispered.

Mrs. Crieff appeared outside and held her keys up.

"Ready?" she asked.

"Come back, kiddo," Mr. Crieff said when he carried my bags to the car.

He loaded everything into the trunk, then came over and folded me into one of his huge hugs. "Always welcome, Marcie. You know that. We had some problems, but who doesn't? C'mon back and sort a few more out for us, okay?"

I nodded and Mrs. Crieff backed the car onto the driveway. Across the street, Vickie's front door opened and she ran down the steps. In one hand, she held a sheet of paper, a pen in the other.

"Wait. Gimme your email address, Marcie, I'll write."

I wrote down my name, then printed, Marcie Beaucoup, in brackets. I copied out my email address and phone number for Vickie.

Vickie, Kevin and Daniella stood on the lawn and waved as Mrs. Crieff and I backed onto the curb. I sat sideways, straining to see as long as I could. It was hard to leave.

When we turned the corner, I stopped waving, leaned my head against the window and groaned. I scarcely spoke all the way downtown, concentrating instead on the scenery. Blue sky. Gray bricks. Red light. I felt like I was on a little outing to an execution or something. When we drove into the lot at Central Station, Mrs. Crieff patted my hand.

"Toronto's not that far, Marcie," she said.

We walked side-by-side through the station, reading the signs beside each track, looking for one marked Toronto. I glanced up at the far wall and saw the history of the city portrayed in small, evenly shaped ceramic tiles. The fur traders. Early settlers. The birth of a city. So much of my own history was in Montreal. And a lot of it had happened since I'd arrived eight weeks ago.

I glanced at Mrs. Crieff, remembering our talk the night Renée had died. Daniella really was lucky.

A crowd waited at the steps leading to the Toronto train and we took our place in line.

"Do you have your ticket, Marcie?" Mrs. Crieff asked again. I nodded, shoving my violin case along with the side of my foot as the line advanced toward the gate. I'd be getting on the train soon, leaving Montreal.

"It feels as though I am saying goodbye to my own daughter, Marcie. The house will seem empty without you."

I wished I could think of something to answer. I had so much to tell her. So much to thank her for that I scarcely knew where to start. The Crieffs' house had once again become my second home. I wanted to let Mrs. Crieff know how much that meant to me. How much she meant to me.

At the top of the cement stairs, I threw my arms around her neck, my cheek against hers. That's when it came to me. Suddenly, I knew exactly what to say and just how to tell her how important she was. I hugged her again.

"Thanks, Adèle," I said.

A girl about my age sat beside me on the train. She looked out the window for a long time. As our train inched out of the station, the girl faced me.

"This is the first time I've ever gone anywhere by myself. It's so exciting. Are you from Montreal?" she asked.

"Yep, I was born here," I answered. "But now I live with my dad in Toronto. I'm going home."

ABOUT THE AUTHOR

Catherine Goodwin is a writer and teacher living in London, Ontario. Like her character Marcie Chisholm, Catherine was born in Montreal and a large part of her own history took place in that city. As a young Montrealer, Catherine visited Expo, watched the Montreal Canadiens play hockey, and skied in the mountains north of the city. She met her husband when he attended the Montreal Olympic Games. Catherine lived in southern California for several years before returning to Canada with her family. She is the author of several short stories, including "The Ballot," published in the Ronsdale young adult anthology, *Beginnings: Stories of Canada's Past* (2001). *Seeking Shelter* is Catherine's first contemporary young adult novel.